EARL OF SIN

LORDS OF SCANDAL

TAMMY ANDRESEN

Keep up with all the latest news, sales, freebies, and releases by joining my newsletter!

www.tammyandresen.com

Hugs!

CHAPTER ONE

MISS MARY CHASE stood at the front gate of the stately mansion situated in the heart of London and stared up at the imposing brick façade. It wasn't too late to turn around, go back to her aunt and uncle's, resume her life.

Lord and Lady Winthrop had taken her in after the loss of her parents seven years ago, even financed a season for her. But she could not, in good conscience, continue to leech off them with no prospect of marriage.

Her aunt insisted she could still find a husband but Mary knew how these things worked. In all likelihood, she'd get passed by. She was four and twenty, after all. No man would want her now. A season would be the exclamation point on the sentence of her life. *You weren't meant for a happily ever after, Mary! Haven't you learned that yet?*

And so instead of another season, she'd accepted an interview for the position of tutor within the home of the Earl of Sinclair.

Her family was mildly appalled. Unlike many girls who'd become orphans, she'd been treated with love and kindness and she'd happily acted as companion to several of her cousins. But she was of age now, and, in her mind, that meant that she ceased to be a burden to them and learned how to care for herself. Besides, she liked being useful. In a life that had been filled with loss, she found real joy in work.

She straightened her shoulders as she approached the front steps. She'd not lose her resolve now. After fixing the ribbons on her bonnet, she raised her hand and lifted the knocker, giving two decisive smacks to the brass plate on the door.

The sound echoed through the house and her insides quivered along with the noise. But she'd gone too far now to back down, so she held her breath as she waited for the door to open.

When her lungs were near bursting, the door swung in, and a tall butler with an amazingly erect back, stared down at her. "Yes?"

Mary swallowed, pressing her hands together. "I'm here for the position of tutor." The earl's daughter, as she understood it, had lost her mother some time ago and the earl wished for a woman of society to teach his daughter how to properly behave. As a spinster who had grown up in the house of an earl, she was perfect for such a task.

The butler's mouth turned down. "I thought you would enter by the kitchen door." He gave her a long look up and down.

Drat. Her chest tightened. She was no longer a member of the family but a servant. How could she have forgotten that? The look on the butler's face assured her he was wondering the same. She dropped into a quick courtesy. Here, the butler was above her in station. "Of course. My apologies."

He gave her a single nod, his expression unchanged. "His lord is expecting you. Follow me."

Her stomach twisted into an uncomfortable knot and she drew in a deep breath to calm it. Mary would not allow her nerves to get the better of her. She had a multitude of family to rely on should this position fall through. She needn't be worried.

Today felt like the beginning of her new life. One where she was independent and able to care for herself. If she failed, she'd be proving she couldn't even complete the simple task of providing for her own future. If she couldn't do that, what could she do exactly? Of what use was she to this world?

The butler started up the stairs and she followed. She'd expected some sort of introduction. When none came, in her usual fashion, she began it herself. "My name is Mary Chase," she murmured, unsure of what else to say. "It's a pleasure to meet you."

"I know," he answered, not looking back. "Should you succeed in this interview, I shall introduce you to the staff."

She pressed her lips together. Apparently, the man wasn't going to perform the basic nicety of giving his name without first making certain she would stay. She had the distinct impression he didn't like her, but why? He didn't even know her.

They reached the top of the stairs and Mary followed him down a lovely hallway, lined with beautifully polished oak panels and covered in thick carpet that dulled their footsteps until they reached an open door.

The butler stepped inside while she remained in the hall. "Miss Chase is here to see you."

"Send her in," a deep male voice replied.

The sound reverberated through her in the most pleasant way. Both strong and capable, she wanted to sigh just hearing those three short words.

The butler turned back to her and waved her forward, with a flick of his hand.

Straightening her back again, she stepped into the room as the butler moved to the side. But she didn't bother to look at him, instead studying the earl. The first thing she noted was the dark crown of his hair as he bent at the desk, finishing some task with his quill. His hair was a touch overlong, which suited him nicely. Rich brown waves swept back from his forehead and down his neck, nearly brushing the nape of his neck. But his hair was forgotten as she noted the breadth of his shoulders, strength of his arms, and the large capable hands that held the tiny quill.

Then he looked up, smiling at her. Chocolate colored eyes and classically handsome nose and cheeks gave way to a strong jaw and lips...dear lord, his lips were the most kissable she'd ever encountered. Even more so than her former fiancé Steven's had been. The

3

thought shocked her and parched her throat. Then air rushed from her lungs as his voice echoed through her again.

"Miss Chase, I presume? It's a pleasure to meet you. The Duke of Darlington has spoken very highly of your abilities. My daughter is in desperate need of aid."

Dear lord, she was in trouble. So very much.

———

LORD COLBERT SINCLAIR, or Sin as his friends called him, assessed the woman in front of him, noting that she was far prettier than he'd prefer. In fact, she was stunning. Daring hadn't mentioned that fact when he'd suggested Mary as a potential tutor.

He'd expected a woman who was older, matronly. She'd have greying hair, with a few wrinkles about the eyes that gave her a kind look. Perhaps she'd be a bit thick in the middle, which would make her excellent for the sort of hugs small girls needed.

The woman before him now embodied none of these attributes. A petite blonde, she had eyes the color of the sky on a clear, bright summer day and the sort of small features that gave her an air of delicate beauty. The last thing he wished for was a woman of beauty in the house.

His first wife had been beautiful. Petite like Mary, she'd brought out every protective instinct Sin possessed. In fact, Mary's resemblance to Clara was rather alarming. Not in the details, of course, but the build, the hair.

He'd loved his wife dearly and had tried to shield her from this harsh world. That was until he couldn't protect her. His insides clenched as he mentally pushed the feeling aside. He didn't need another woman to keep safe. He'd already failed at that task once with his wife and now he had a daughter who worried him constantly. More so of late.

Besides, she was here for a teaching position, not as a candidate for his hand. And to that end, he'd wanted an elderly matron to love Anne, not a woman who was young enough to be her mother. That was essential. Mary, connected in society and beautiful as she was, would likely only be a temporary figure in their lives. He needed someone stable and constant in Anne's life.

And certainly not a woman so lovely.

"It's a pleasure to meet you as well, my lord," she murmured, dropping into a curtsey. "Thank you for granting me this interview."

He grimaced. Daring had left out some key facts. Likely on purpose. But Mary was here now, he might as well conduct the interview. Anne had been a precocious child up to a few months ago. A mad woman had stolen her from his home and since then, his lovely daughter had grown fearful and had retreated into a shell. Or perhaps, he had grown overprotective and pushed her into one. "It is my pleasure." He gestured toward the chair. "Please. Have a seat." Either way, he needed the right person to draw her out again. There was a kindness in Mary's eyes that suited the position and he was tempted to hire her, but something else held him back. What if Anne grew attached to the woman? Just like him, his daughter had suffered loss. He didn't want to put either of them through that again.

She did as he instructed, her back straight as she stared at a spot on his desk. "Thank you."

"Tell me. Have you ever tutored a young girl before?"

She nodded. "I've lived with my aunt and uncle since I was sixteen. Grace was only nine." Her hands tightened into a knot on her lap. "Not quite as young as your daughter but I can assure you, Grace was a handful."

Sin smiled. "I've met her. I have to agree." He cleared his throat. "And your education?"

Her gaze was still fixed somewhere below his. "I was a student as Lady Kitteridge's School of Comportment. My marks were excellent."

He drew in a long breath. That was excellent news. While he wished for his daughter to regain her confidence, he did not want to sacrifice her future as a lady. Much as he hated to admit it, Mary suited the position well in that regard. "Did you attend a season?"

"One," she answered, her features tightening.

He cocked his head to the side, assessing her. "Why just one?" With her uncle being an earl, surely she could have had several. Could still decide to rejoin society and find a fitting husband.

"I was engaged to the second son of the Earl of Everly, but he was lost in the Napoleonic Wars four years ago."

He gripped his quill harder. Bloody hell that was rough. Almost as terrible as his own story. "I'm sorry for your loss. You didn't see fit to reenter society?"

She shook her head. "No, my lord."

"And you're leaving your aunt and uncle's house because?"

Her eyes rose to his then. They crinkled at the corners in a bit of sadness. He understood it completely. His stomach tightened in understanding and, if he were honest, attraction. Not a feeling he welcomed. "My cousins have all married and no longer need a companion. I can't justify being a dependent in my uncle's house if I am not serving a purpose there."

He straightened, appreciation making his chin tuck back. "Surely, he would continue to support you."

Her delicate shoulders rose then fell. The curve of them was lovely and his fingers itched to trace their slender shape. "I'm sure he would. But I will not be a burden to my family any more than I've already been. I'm perfectly capable of working."

He blinked. He had to confess, for her small stature she was decidedly determined. He liked that. Honestly, he liked her.

Which was dangerous. She'd be his employee, which meant he needed to remain detached from her. Besides, she looked strikingly like his first wife and that was the type of woman he'd never touch again.

CHAPTER TWO

MARY PRESSED her hands together in her lap, hoping the desk covered her gesture. She wanted to appear confident despite the fact she was anything but.

She'd like to blame her nerves over embarking on a new chapter in her life but even she knew her fluttering stomach was caused in part by his warmly handsome façade. She looked down into her lap. "Perhaps I should introduce you to my daughter. See how the two of you get on."

She nodded, still not looking up. Part of her wished to rise from the chair, thank him for the interview, and leave. She could return home but her pride demanded she stay. She'd never intended to be a spinster but this was her life now and she'd make the best of it she could. "That's an excellent idea."

"Reeves," Lord Sinclair called. "Would you fetch Anne? She's waiting in the nursery."

"Of course, my lord," the butler answered, his voice rising as though quite happy to complete the task. He sounded like a completely different man then the one who'd greeted her at the door.

She snapped her teeth together to keep from sighing. Mr. Reeves was going to be terrible to work with if the Earl hired her.

"I'm glad you're here." Sinclair pulled her from her thoughts. "We've had a difficult few months and I'll be glad for the help."

"Difficult?" she asked, her chin snapping up. Which was a mistake. Those eyes drew her in the moment their gazes met.

Sinclair frowned as he rubbed his forehead. "Are you aware of the special circumstances that Lady Abernath created?"

Mary's lips pursed. The Countess of Abernath had died but before she did, she'd made the Chase lives a living hell. Mary herself had been knocked out when the other woman had stolen her cousin, Cordelia. "Yes, of course. I too suffered at her hand."

The quill in Sinclair's hand snapped. "She stole my daughter from our back alley in her plot to try and get to your cousin, Diana. My daughter hasn't been the same since the kidnapping."

Mary drew in a gasp. "Poor child."

He rubbed his neck. "It was my intention to marry but with everything in such turmoil, I just don't know if that's wise. Anne, however, she needs help now. She's terrified after what happened." He raked his hand through his hair. "She mostly appears fine during the day but at night..."

Mary's heart jumped in her throat. She remembered her own sense of helplessness when she'd been knocked out and Ada had been taken. No wonder the child was afraid. "Of course she does," she murmured. "Truly, if that's what you're hoping for, I'm sure I can help you. I understand the threat and I helped my own family cope. I—" She stopped, sure she was saying too much.

His eyebrows had lifted and he stared at her for a few moments before he finally spoke. "With all due respect, you dealt with this as a grown woman. She is a child. One who already lost her mother."

A flush filled her cheeks, heating her skin. He had every right to protect his daughter by choosing the best woman for this position. "As I said, I've worked with children and have intimate knowledge of the situation with Lady Abernath. I think I could help you."

"My lord," Reeves called from the door. "Lady Anne."

Mary stood, as did Lord Sinclair, and she turned toward the door to see a darling girl assessing her. Large brown eyes exactly like her father's blinked back at Mary.

"Anne," her father called. "This is Miss Chase. She's applying for the position of your tutor."

The little girl gave a curtsey. "Pleased to meet you."

"And you as well." Mary gave the girl what she hoped was a warm smile. She noted the girl was perfectly dressed, her hair impeccably groomed into symmetrical ringlets and her shoes nicely polished. "Don't you look lovely."

The girl grimaced, her hands lifting out her skirt. "My nanny helps me ready for the day."

Inwardly, Mary cringed. She wondered if the butler had hired the nanny. The girl looked as stuffy as Reeves acted. Granted, Anne was the daughter of an earl but a child should be exploring and having fun, she wasn't just a doll to dress up. And she'd gain confidence by playing outdoors. "I see. And what do you do with your day?"

The girl looked to her father, nibbling on her lip. "I have lessons, I read, and practice the pianoforte."

Outwardly, Mary gave the girl a glowing smile, inwardly she grimaced. The child was too young for such a busy schedule. "And I bet you are excellent at all your lessons."

The child shook her head. "I'm not very good at music."

Lord Sinclair cleared his throat. "You just need practice."

Mary didn't look at him. It was dangerous considering the heat that filled her every time she glanced his way. But, standing here with Anne, she was glad she hadn't run. This child needed help and she'd thought of a few ways to give it. "And perhaps some inspiration."

The little girl looked at Mary, her eyes growing wider and brighter. "Inspiration?"

Mary nodded. "One of my cousins is a wonderful pianoforte player, another a painter, a third plays the flute."

"Painting." The girl clasped her hands, bobbing on her heels. "How fun."

Lord Sinclair cleared his throat. "It does indeed sound very entertaining. But we've a schedule to keep. For now, why don't you return to your lessons?"

Mary held her breath. What did that mean? Had she failed this portion of the interview? Did she actually want to work here? This little girl desperately needed her help. Not only had the child had a traumatic experience but she was being crushed by a schedule. Stiffening her spine, she looked back at Lord Sinclair. It was time to fight for the position.

———

SIN LOOKED BACK AT MARY, his chest tightening. Having this woman under his roof was a terrible idea. Even now, she nibbled her lip, giving him a questioning glance. Something about her vulnerability called to him. He didn't want a woman like this tempting him daily. There were times he thought he might never want a woman again. And Anne needed someone with an infinite amount of caring and kindness, which was why she likely wasn't right for the position.

Then again, he'd be a fool not to acknowledge that Anne already liked Mary and vice versa. Hell, he hadn't seen Anne smile like that in months. Damn. Damn. Damn.

Drawing in a deep breath, he clenched a fist at his side. If he hired her, he'd just have to control himself. Ignore her little upturned nose and generous lips. Forget the ivory tone of her skin that looked kissed by pink roses in all the right places. The apples of her cheeks, for example. And those lips.

His nickname was Sin, and before his first wife, he'd been quite the rake. Not now. Now he was a lord and a father, and a man drowning in life's problems and responsibilities. But back then, he'd seen his fair share of women with their clothes off. Which meant he knew with certainty that her nipples would be that same shade of frost pink and...he stopped himself. What the bloody hell was wrong with him?

His attraction was already clouding his judgement. She wasn't at all what he'd wanted and he still wasn't certain she was the best woman for the job.

Swallowing, he leaned his hands onto the desk. "I have to confess, I'd hoped for someone older, more experienced for the position."

She pressed her lips together, her hands gripped tightly in front of her. "I'm sure I can do the job if you'd let me try."

He raised a brow. Try? Anne needed security, not attempts. Especially if they failed. Then again, Daring had recommended her. "Perhaps I could hire you on a trial basis? Maybe a fortnight. We can see how you and Anne work together." And if he could tolerate having her in the house.

"Of course," she murmured as she scooted closer, moving out to the end of her chair. Even a few weeks could give her the opportunity to get to know the girl, make some changes. "I'd love the opportunity. When would you like me to start? I just need a bit of time to collect a few necessities. That won't take more than a day."

"Good," he answered, straightening again. "Then I shall send a carriage for you first thing in the morning."

She gave a stiff nod. "May I ask…" She twisted her gloved fingers together. "What do you see as my duties?"

That was a question that did not fill him with confidence and clenched his jaw tighter. "Your duties are to care for her. Support her to help her feel better. Daring said you're quite good at encouraging young ladies to reach their potential."

She nodded. "Perhaps I should ask when I complete those duties. What does her daily schedule entail?"

He frowned. "I see your point. It's quite full. I thought keeping her busy might distract her from her worries."

She nodded. "She'll need lessons, but I'll need time with her too. And perhaps a different wardrobe."

"Wardrobe?" Her assertion made his head snap back. He forgot all about her fragile appearance, his attraction and his desire to protect her. "Her clothes are impeccable."

Mary nodded. "I quite agree. Lovely."

He relaxed for a moment glad that they understood one another. His daughter was a lovely child and he supposed he liked to see that beauty highlighted. It would have been a mother's job but he thought he had taken the task on admirably.

Then Mary continued. "However, I need her to have clothes that she can get dirty."

He nearly fell back into his chair. Was she questioning his parental decisions already? Had he just made a mistake hiring this woman? He'd done so against his better judgment and that never worked to his advantage. "I don't think you understand what I'm looking for. I like that she is well-mannered, well-dressed, refined."

Mary licked her lips and for a moment, he forgot his point entirely, then she stepped closer to the desk, her hands rising in front of her. "Hear me out. A girl who sits quietly studying and never gets dirty isn't going to become braver. She needs…." Dear lord, she did it again. Mary's pretty pink tongue swiped across her lips. "She needs to do challenging things and become more confident."

His brows drew together. "She does challenging things. Pianoforte, for example."

It was Mary's turn to lean across the desk. "The thing she doesn't think she's very good at? That is going to make her more confident? Less afraid?"

Bloody hell, that was a rather good point. His insides relaxed a hair. "What will then?"

Mary shrugged. "That's what I need time to discover." She gave him a hopeful smile. "Do you think I could have her in the afternoons?"

His mouth dropped. "All afternoon?" He shook his head. What had he done?

She squared her shoulders. "What did you have in mind?"

"I don't know. Between pianoforte and Latin." He waved his hand. "In other words, when she isn't in other lessons."

Mary cocked her head to one side. "You want to fill more of her schedule? Do you think by doing so, she won't have time to be frightened? And honestly, you've hired me on a temporary basis to prove myself but don't want to give me any time to actually do the job. I'm destined to fail."

That irritated him. Mary might look like a slender flower but she was acting like a prickly thorn bush. He leaned down to make certain his eyes were level with hers. "You've been in my employ for less than a minute and you're already insulting my parenting?"

CHAPTER THREE

MARY REALIZED her mistake and she drew back from the desk as though the wood had scalded her. "Apologies, my lord." She dipped into a curtsey. "I am used to being a member of the family." She'd have to learn to be an employee. But if she were going to help Anne, Lord Sinclair would also have to figure out how to hand over some measure of control. His ways weren't working. "If you would see fit to keep me in your employ, even for this trial basis, I can assure you, I will learn my place." If he fired her, she'd have to crawl back to her aunt and uncle's home. She'd be a failure in every way then. Unwed and unemployable. She'd grown accustomed to the fact she wouldn't have a fairy-tale ending but was she doomed to be a complete failure in life? If only her tongue were less sharp. But she could hardly change who she was now. And perhaps her strength would benefit Anne.

"It's not my feelings I'm concerned about, but my daughter's. The question is, can you help her?" He scrubbed his neck, his features tight with worry.

She pressed her hands down her skirts, brushing out the invisible wrinkles. She was a Chase woman through and through and her opinions could be overwhelming at times. She'd have to work harder to keep them in check. This wasn't the first time it had gotten her into significant trouble. "I can, my lord. After everything I've been through, for better or worse, it's only made me less compromising. Stronger. It's that kind of strength Anne must find within herself."

HE CAME around the desk and another fear caused her to take a half step back. Without the desk between them, he seemed even larger. Long, powerful legs and a lean torso making his shoulders seem even broader. She cleared her throat, attempting to remove a lump.

"There's no need to be nervous. I consider myself a fair and reasonable man." He reached out to her and then dropped his hand again.

"That's very generous." She tightened her fingers in the fabric while looking over his shoulder rather than directly at him. It occurred to her again that this interview was a mistake. So she had to return home? She'd be safe from this attraction and her own flaws that always seem to crop up and cause problems for her. But then what? Live the rest of her life as a guest in her uncle's home with no purpose in life? "Thank you."

He nodded quickly. "I shall see you tomorrow then."

"Tomorrow," she murmured before turning to flee. That was the only word for her spinning exit.

Back in her uncle's carriage, she slumped down into the seat. The little girl was delightful. Mary would truly enjoy trying to help the child. But Lord Sinclair… Sin, she'd heard Darlington and Lord Viceroy call him, he was…distracting.

A very handsome distraction. Her eyes drifted closed. Only one other man had ever tempted her the way Sin had. The honorable Harold Marksby, son of the Earl of Everly and her fiancé. He'd been tall and so broad in the shoulders that she'd made a habit of tracing the outline of them from his neck down to his arms.

She sighed to herself. She'd allowed Harold all sorts of liberties because of those shoulders. And, of course, because of his proposal.

Once they'd been engaged to be married, well, they'd been granted time alone. She brought her hands up to cover her face. Thinking back on it, she wished she'd allowed him more. They'd kissed and touched and teased in ways that had made her ache.

Unfortunately, he had little inheritance of his own and wanting to provide for her, he'd left for the army. That's when her Chase temper had gotten the best of her. She'd railed at him. She'd rather be poor and have him at her side than be rich with him gone to France. But he shook his head and told her that she didn't understand a man's job. He was the provider. How could he be her husband if he didn't provide?

She'd hit him in the chest, rather hard, and asked how he planned to provide if he was gone?

That was the last words they'd spoken. In the end, she wished she'd been more flexible and given herself to him, wished that she'd kissed him farewell with tears in her eyes and proclaimed her undying love. Instead, she'd sent him off with angry words and hurt feelings. What a fool she was.

And she'd nearly lost her position today. But she'd been granted just enough time to prove herself, her worth. She leaned her head against the wood frame of the carriage. Years had passed since she'd lost Harry. She'd mourned his death for a long time. Been too grief stricken to move on. She no longer felt sad about Harry. Instead, she wished she'd listened to her aunt when she'd urged her to rejoin society to go out and find another man to wed.

Because Mary would have no husband now, no family of her own. A woman of four and twenty was firmly on the shelf. But she could still be useful. Have purpose. It was some consolation. Soon her cousins would start having babies. Once Anne no longer needed her, she could go work for one of them to help to raise their children.

That made her sit back up. She had a plan and it was a good one. The best she could do.

The carriage pulled up to her aunt and uncle's drive just as another carriage rolled in behind her. Peeking out of the curtain, she smiled as she saw Lord Viceroy's carriage. Her cousin, Ada, had come to visit.

Mary gave a small clap as she exited the carriage and stood on the path to wait for Ada to exit. Her cousin was a quiet and thoughtful woman, unlike most of the Chases, who would surely have advice for Mary on how to be her most subdued self. She needed to keep her tongue in check, at least for the next few weeks until she was given the position full time.

But Mary's excitement dampened as Lord Viceroy stepped out first to help his wife down. While Mary was glad the two were so enamored with one another, Mary herself would have liked a visit with just Ada.

"Hello," Vice called, waving. "How did the interview with Sin go?"

Sin and Vice were first cousins and had been close as children. "Anne is a wonderful little girl," she answered, not wanting to discuss her own failings or Sin's.

Vice grinned. "Indeed, she is."

Ada stepped up to hug Anne. "Lord Sinclair will be lucky to have your help."

Mary's lips pressed together, but she didn't respond. The fact that he'd given her such a small window made her think that he didn't really trust her to help. She'd prove him wrong. "I will be fortunate to gain the position."

Ada narrowed her gaze, her chin notching to the side. "Mary, you are a wonderful caregiver. Anyone can see that."

"Thank you, Ada," she answered, linking her arm with the other woman's. "Let's go see your parents. They've missed you."

Ada began walking with her. "How did you like Lord Sinclair?"

Mary's feet faltered, and she tripped on nothing at all. "Fine," she answered in a croak. How did she say that she was both terribly attracted to the man and sure she herself had been off-putting to say the least?

"Fine?" Ada asked slowing their pace further. "What does that mean precisely?"

"Ada." She gave her cousin's arm a squeeze. "It means the interview went well and I begin the position tomorrow." *At least for now.* But

Mary refrained from sharing that thought so as not to worry Ada as she looked over at Vice. "Lord Viceroy, do you consider your cousin to be a man of even temperament?"

"Indeed," Vice answered, but Ada pursed her lips, frowning.

"Chad," Ada murmured. "Perhaps you should take this time to visit with your own family while I see mine."

"What?" he asked stopping on the steps. "Why can't I come with you today and then you come with me tomorrow?"

Ada cleared her throat. "I wish to shop tomorrow. I'll walk you back to the carriage. Mary," Ada turned to look at her. "Why don't you wait for me in the front parlor? I'll be right there."

Mary gave a nod even as her insides clenched. She'd wanted to talk with Ada alone and she'd get her wish, but somehow, she knew that Ada was about to begin stirring the pot.

———

SIN SAT AT HIS DESK, staring at nothing in particular. His thoughts were focused quite firmly on the woman who had left his home an hour before. He'd fetched a new quill, though he'd yet to dip the device in ink.

Part of him was tempted to write a letter to Mary Chase explaining that while she appeared to be of excellent family and skill, she simply wasn't right for his household. His mouth twisted into a frown. The truth was, she might very well be right about and for Anne. The person she wasn't correctly fitted to was himself. He scrubbed his face. At least this was all temporary. He could let her go after that two-week test.

The thought of her being fitted to him once again made all his muscles tense. Damn his willful body and its desire for fragile beauty. But that was only part of the problem. She'd come in and in a rather strong move, had begun pointing out his flaws, of which he had many. Hell, he knew he was failing Anne. He knew that despite wearing those proper dresses and pristine bows, his daughter wasn't happy. And Mary had recognized the problem instantly.

Which was why he needed to give her a chance.

The parchment in front of him remained empty. Could Mary make the difference in his daughter's life?

"My lord," Reeves called from the door, his nasally voice penetrating Sin's reflections. "Lord Viceroy is here to see you. He has arrived unannounced yet again."

His head snapped up. Vice? "Send him in."

The butler pursed his lips. "Yes, my lord."

Sin sat back in his chair. What did Vice want? But then he tossed the quill on the desk. The question didn't need asking. Vice was certainly here to find out how the interview had gone with Mary. Likely Vice's wife had sent him to discuss how the interview went.

Vice walked through the door, wearing his usual devil-may-care look. His arms swung at his side and there was a bit of bounce to his step.

"I see marriage has done little to dampen your spirit." He looked at Vice, who took the seat across from Sin, lounging back without a care.

"Marriage dampen my spirit?" Vice winked. "I'm the happiest I have been in…" Vice looked at the ceiling. "Forever."

Jealousy tore through Sin's chest. "How fortunate for you."

The smile slipped from Vice's face. "Your turn for happiness is coming again soon, cousin. I've no doubt."

Sin shook his head. Falling in love meant making one's self far too vulnerable. "Thank you for saying so. I'm not sure I even strive for happiness. Stability would suit me fine."

Vice winced. "You have achieved that financially."

"I have. And with help from you that I appreciate more than I could say. Now if I could just get Anne on the right path, I would consider myself content."

Vice sat straight in his chair. "So you've decided to hire Mary to help you then."

Sin grimaced. He couldn't hide it. "I did. But…" He didn't know quite how to express his hesitation and the employment probation he'd decreed.

Vice leaned his elbows on his knees. "You trusted me when I told you I could help you financially. Taking over the club has given you the funds to hire the staff you need. Now trust me when I say that Mary can help your daughter. She's got an intuition with these sorts of things that can't be explained."

Sin let out a long breath. "She hadn't been here five minutes when she questioned my parenting choices."

Vice sat back in his chair, his lips pulling up at the corners. "Ah, yes. Don't you love their feisty spirit? The Chase women are quite the handful and I mean that both figuratively and—"

"Thank you," Sin cut him off, not needing to add to his visual picture of the woman. "You're talking about a potential member of my staff."

"I was talking about my wife, actually." Vice winked. "But you shouldn't be afraid of strong-willed staff. Your butler is a beast."

His butler was, in fact, a rather opinionated man. But not when it came to the areas that Sin was actually vulnerable. And besides, Reeves' strength was part of what had carried him through the past few years. Right or wrong, he'd needed the man. "He keeps the rest of the staff in check."

Vice raised a brow. "He's too familiar."

Sin stood, crossing to the fire. "So your point is that I should hire more people to push me around?"

Vice chuckled. "Well said. And no. Mary is a good woman and she'll learn her place. In the meantime, Anne will only benefit from the Chase strength of character."

"Is she strong?" Sin murmured. "Mary that is. She looks so—"

"Beautiful?" Vice asked.

Sin turned back to Vice, the other man's eyes sparkling with mischief. "I was going to say delicate. Fragile. Perhaps..." The sort of woman Sin might grow attached to. His chest ached with the pain of the past.

Vice shook his head. "Don't let her size fool you. Strength of character comes from within."

That was a bloody good point. "If you truly think she'll help Anne, then she's worth trying."

Vice winked again, his hand lacing behind his head. "I think she'll do a world of good in this house."

Sin assessed his cousin, his thoughts twisting about in his head. Did Vice also think he was failing Anne? And even if Mary was the answer, how would he survive their cohabitation?

CHAPTER FOUR

MARY STOOD as Ada entered the room. "You didn't need to send Vice away."

"Yes, I did." She pushed up her glasses and stopped just in front of Mary. "Tell me what's wrong."

Mary looked at the wall to her right. Words filled her mouth, wishing to spill all her worries to Ada but then again, Ada might tell Vice, who might then share with Sin. "Nothing is wrong."

"Liar," Ada reached for her hand. "You're upset."

Mary rubbed her temples, shaking her head. "I insulted his parenting right to his face," she whispered. "Lord Sinclair almost didn't hire me. As it is, he's going to bring me on for a fortnight to test out the arrangement."

"A fortnight?" Ada squeezed her fingers. "I like Lord Sinclair a great deal, but he needs major help in the parenting department and I am so glad you're able to give it to him. Even if he might not keep you on permanently. Though if anyone can convince him to change, it's you."

"What?" Mary looked at Ada.

Ada pursed her lips. "That child needs a little freedom to overcome her fears."

Warmth spread through Mary. "That's exactly what I thought."

Ada nodded. "He's grief-stricken from the loss of his wife. He can't see that path. But you'll aid them both. I'm sure of it."

Mary's eyes widened. "I don't know, Ada. I don't think he liked me." Mary didn't add that she liked him far more than was proper. Like wasn't exactly the word. She was drawn to him in a way she had never experienced before. The tips of her fingers tingled to touch his hair, and she'd spent far too long wondering what it'd be like to share an intimate embrace with him. Shivers trickled down her spine. Maybe more than an embrace…

"How could he not like you?" Ada wrapped her arms about Mary. "You're smart and fun and full of zest." Her cousin gave her a squeeze.

"Thank you," Mary gave Ada a hug before stepping back. "I appreciate your words of comfort."

"But you're not comforted," Ada added, her hands coming to her hips. Slowly she looked Mary up and down as though she were studying for clues. "Something else is bothering you."

"No," Mary yelped but even she knew she'd said it far too quickly and much too loudly.

Ada slowly adjusted her spectacles on her nose. "It's his looks, isn't it?"

"What?" Heat filled her cheeks. "No. Of course it isn't."

Ada shook her head, waving her off. Of course her cousin didn't believe her. "They're distracting. One man shouldn't be allowed to be so handsome."

Mary's shoulders slumped. "The same could be said for your husband."

Ada tapped her chin. "True. But I wasn't considering living full time as his employee."

Mary shrugged. "I'll have to keep my head down and keep to myself, I guess."

Ada turned and walked toward the window. "I say you be yourself. You would do him a world of good. And for that matter you could also apply yourself to marrying him."

Mary gasped. "I'm the tutor. And a spinster and—"

23

"From good family, beautiful, motherly, and available." Ada turned back, a flicker of interest sparkling in her eyes. "This could be your chance to have a family of your own. You don't say it but you feel the call. I've seen you around infants."

Mary couldn't deny her deepest yearnings, slumping in her chair, resting her head in her hands. "If I wanted the position of wife, I probably should have made a more favorable impression on the interview."

Ada covered her mouth with her hand, suppressing a chuckle. "Oh Mary. That is a bit funny."

Mary shrugged. "And true."

"Funny things often are." Ada came back to her side, laying a hand on her shoulder. "But your chance isn't finished. Prove yourself valuable and see how your future unfolds." Ada took a step away but then came back. "And protect your virtue. He'll have to marry you if he wants that."

That made Mary's head snap up. "He doesn't want me that way at all." She might be ridiculously attracted to him but he'd been the picture of control.

"Oh please. You're stunning and just his type, or at least that's what Vice says." Ada gave her a sideways glance.

Just his type? Was that true? "What sort is that?"

Ada shrugged then waved her hand. "Lovely, petite. You might be surprised by how much he actually likes you."

MARY SAT BACK in her chair. But why would he have been so cold if he'd been interested in her?

———

SIN STOOD JUST outside the front door, Anne's hand tucked into his. In the end they'd decided to give her a few days off from lessons to get to know Mary. Might as well give her trial run a real chance at success. They'd also agreed to greet Mary when she arrived to make her feel welcome.

Which was a decision he wanted to regret. Lords did not, as a general rule, meet staff at the door on their first day. But as Anne bounced next to him, the first real smile on her lips that he'd seen in weeks, he had a difficult time regretting the choice.

"What do you think we'll do?" Anne asked, dancing a bit on the end of his hand. She reminded him of a kite on a string. "Do you think we'll go to see her cousins?"

"I don't know," he answered, watching for the carriage. Was it wrong that he couldn't wait to have another look at her?

Anne gave another wiggle. "I'd like to see the ships at the docks."

He crinkled his brow, looking down at his daughter. "Miss Chase is here to teach you to be a lady, not a hooligan."

Ann immediately stilled. "Yes, Papa."

He winced. He hadn't meant to spoil her good mood. "That doesn't mean you won't have fun. In fact, Mary seems to think a bit of adventure would be good for you."

Anne's eyes lit again. "I can't wait."

He tightened his jaw, grinding his teeth together. How had Mary come in and instantly known what his daughter needed when he didn't have a clue. Perhaps he'd been preoccupied—at first, to keep his business afloat. Then, saving Anne from the countess, and at last, dealing with her after the traumatic kidnapping. Hopefully, he'd given Mary enough time to find out.

The carriage rumbled through the gates and started up the drive, making its way toward them. Anne gripped his hand tightly, holding her breath, and he had the urge to do the same. As the carriage ground to a halt, the driver climbed down and snapped open the door. Then Mary, lifting her skirts, climbed down from the vehicle. His breath caught as he glimpsed her slender ankle.

The skirts fell into place and Anne bolted forward, throwing her arms wide. "Miss Chase, Miss Chase you're here! What shall we do today?"

Mary caught his daughter up in a hug. "The possibilities are endless," she replied, running her hand down Anne's braid. As requested, she'd been dressed in an old gown, the child's hair simply styled. "But why don't you start by showing me to my room?"

Anne let go and clapped. "Wonderful. You're going to stay right next to me."

Mary's snapped her gaze up to his. "Not with the servants?"

He winced, rubbing his hand on the back of his neck. "I suppose I consider your position to be more like a nanny."

Her gaze narrowed. "But she has a nanny already."

"Anne," he should have explained more yesterday. He'd gotten distracted by his attraction to her along with her decidedly strong personality. So different from Clara. "Take Miss Chase's bag upstairs."

"Yes, Papa," Anne said, taking the bag from the driver. "Reeves can help me."

Reeves came down the steps. "I'd be happy to, Miss Anne." He gave the girl a soft grin. "Shall we?" And the two of them headed off, each holding a handle of her bag.

"I didn't expect to see a soft side to that man," Mary said as she watched them go.

Sin shook his head. "He's always been like that with her. He was like that with me too as a child."

Mary stepped up to his side. "That makes a great deal more sense."

"As to why I don't sack him?" Sin smiled, drinking in the details of her face.

She smiled back, so sweet and lovely. "Yes." She stepped next to him. "I assume you wanted to speak with me about the room assignment?"

He nodded as he held out his arm to help her up the steps. She looked down, hesitating. "I'm not a lady that you need to escort."

She was right of course, but he didn't drop his elbow. "We may as well accept the fact that this is not a normal arrangement."

She looked up at him with her lips parted in surprise. She swallowed then asked. "How so?"

Looking down at her like that made him ache with want, and belatedly he realized what his words might have implied. "What I

26

mean is that you are family to my family. And the role I need from you is hardly of a normal teacher."

Mary gave a tentative nod, slipping her hand into the crook of his elbow. "That makes sense."

He started up the stairs. "You should know that Anne has been having nightmares. The nanny has tried everything to get her to sleep through the night but nothing's worked."

"Poor thing," Mary murmured, drawing in a shuddering breath. "So I am next to her to help her at night as well as during the day?"

"If you are willing," he answered. "But even if you're not, we both know you are not a normal servant in this house. A fact I'll share with Reeves as well. I gather from your comment that he was less than friendly yesterday?"

Shaking her head, she looked up to him again. "It doesn't matter. I'm sure he was only being protective of Anne."

Sin stopped in the foyer, turning partially toward her. "He likely was, but it will be my job to protect you as well while you are under my roof. If I don't, my guess is I'll be answering to Vice."

Mary gave him a sidelong glance. "Did he come here yesterday? Was he meddling?" Her fingers tightened about his elbow, her grip rather firm. "Ada put him up to it. I'm sure of it. What did he say? Tell me he didn't embarrass you or me or both of us?"

Sin opened his mouth, not sure what to say. What did she mean by embarrass? But he didn't get a chance to ask as Anne returned back down the stairs. "Mary," she bounced in front of her new tutor. "Would you like to come see your room."

Mary's hand slipped from his arm. He should be happy that Anne was so elated but some part of him missed Mary's touch on his arm.

As she glided gracefully up the stairs, he reminded himself that he didn't need another woman like her complicating his life. But somehow, he couldn't make his body agree.

CHAPTER FIVE

MARY WATCHED the child bounce about the bedroom. Her plan was already working. At least she hoped it was. Her goal was to build Anne's confidence during the day to help her cope with fear at night.

"What shall we do Miss Chase?" the child sang. "Take a great adventure?"

Mary laughed. "Yes. A fantastic one full of adventure, mystery, and activity."

"Where?" Anne bounced on her heels. "Where shall we go?"

Lord Sinclair had implied the child was struggling with fear but thus far, Mary had seen no evidence of that fact. "To the garden," she replied, suppressing a grin when Anne let out a loud groan.

"The garden?"

"Yes. The garden." She crossed the room reaching for one of her bags. "But I think we'll take this with us."

"What is it?" Anne asked her eyes growing larger as she stepped toward Mary.

"Take a look," Mary answered, unclasping the bag.

Anne set the bag on the bed and then opened it slowly, letting out a loud gasp as she looked inside. "They're so beautiful."

Mary gave one of the girl's braids a tug. "I thought you'd like them."

Grace, an accomplished artist, had allowed Mary to raid her art supplies. Sketch books, charcoals, paints, and brushes graced the inside of the bag. "Today I think we'll start with the charcoal and work our way to painting. Next week, Grace will come over to give you some lessons."

Anne let go of the bag to clap wildly as she spun about. "Papa, did you hear? We're going to draw in the garden."

"I heard," Lord Sinclair rumbled from the doorway.

Her entire body tensed at the sound. She hadn't heard him come down the hall, thanks to the carpeting, and she heated as she wondered how long he'd been watching. She turned to face him, straightening in a show of strength that she didn't feel. "Can we picnic for the noon meal as well?"

Anne gasped with delight. "A picnic. Oh, yes, please!" Then she danced over to her father. "Papa. You should picnic with us too. Wouldn't that be fun?"

Inwardly Mary groaned. She came here for Anne and despite her earlier pondering about fulfilling a few fantasies with Lord Sinclair, she'd realized the foolishness of that idea the moment she'd arrived. He was her employer. And she had a future to build.

"It does sound fun, sweetheart." He pushed off the doorframe and entered the room. "If that's all right with Miss Chase?"

"Of course." She nodded, looking at Anne. She was going to have to overcome this attraction or her post would be short-lived. "Will the cook permit us to pack it ourselves before we go out?"

"I'm sure she would but she could pack it for you and I could take it out."

His voice rumbled through her as she continued to watch the girl dance about the room. She was determined not to look at Lord Sinclair while she brought herself back under control.

Swallowing, she drew in a deep breath. "That's quite all right. We'll pack it ourselves." Then she reached for Anne's hand as the girl slipped her fingers into Mary's. "Anne, since your Papa will be our distinguished guest, do you know what he might like to eat or should we ask him?"

Anne crinkled her brow. "He likes chicken. And lamb..." The child looked up to the ceiling. "And meat pies."

Mary gave her an appreciative smile. "Excellent. I bet you can pack him all his favorite things."

Anne nodded eagerly. "Wouldn't that be grand. I'll go tell Cook." And with that the girl darted off.

"Well," Lord Sinclair rumbled as the girl disappeared. "You've certainly got her excited."

Mary nodded. "Indeed."

"Is there a method to all this enthusiasm?" He moved closer. She felt his heat through her clothes. Her fingers clenched into her skirts.

"There is," she answered. "Being useful. Doing for others builds confidence in ourselves." She drew in a deep breath. "And she seems interested in drawing. I want her to be good at things. But..." This made her smile. "For our first days, I thought we would stay on the property. Test out her fears and what drives them."

His hand came up to her shoulder. She hadn't expected it and a shiver raced down her spine at his touch. "Thank you for taking on the position. I'm very hopeful to see what the next few weeks bring."

Heat radiated from her face. "I haven't done anything yet. Reserve your thanks until I've been successful."

He brushed his fingers down her arm. "I see a difference in her already and for my part..." He hesitated. "You were right yesterday. I thought by guiding her on proper presentation for a lady I was doing the job of a mother—"

Her insides twisted. How difficult it must be for him to raise a daughter on his own. "I spoke out of turn and truly, you are a caring and concerned father. She couldn't ask for more."

Silence fell between them, but he didn't move away. In fact, if anything, he drifted closer. Her own breath stalled in her chest. "Thank you," he finally whispered.

"You're welcome," she replied, a lump of nerves clogging her throat. "I should go help Anne." Then, breaking from his side, she lifted her skirts to walk more quickly to the door. She needed a bit of space because wild fantasies of kissing him and Ada's words had begun echoing through her head.

———

MARY WAS GOING to be the death of him. Sin stood in her room and did a slow circle as he assessed her bags and trunk. Nothing had been unpacked, most were neatly stacked under the window where the valet had likely left them.

One sat open on the bed, the very one that had sent Anne into cries of elation. Why hadn't art lessons occurred to him? And picnics?

He'd watched Mary stroke his daughter's braid with gentle fingers and something inside him had shifted. Anne hadn't been this excited in months. Perhaps Mary was just the change that Anne had needed after all.

He found himself leaving the room and heading down the back stairs toward the kitchen. She was breathing life into him too. His insides were a twisting mess, he'd barely slept last night in anticipation of her arrival, and the thought of picnicking with her sounded...delightful.

He stopped on the steps, halfway between the first and second floor. He'd felt this way once before. Clara had been a small woman of fragile beauty. Later he'd learned that she'd spent much of her childhood ill, but as an adult, she'd outgrown the illness.

He'd loved the way she'd fit under his arm, and Mary was right about people finding joy in caring for others. He'd taken great delight in shielding her from the world. Of course, he hadn't been able to do a damn thing about planting his seed in her womb. And he'd been completely helpless when birthing had been too much for her.

His head dropped in his hands. Yes, he felt a pull toward Mary. But she wasn't the type of woman he should marry. The next time, he'd take a wife of strong stock. Though Mary was strong-willed, that still didn't mean she could survive pregnancy and childbirth given her small stature.

Dropping his hands, he continued down to the kitchen. He stopped, watching Mary help Anne cut bread, her hands gently guiding his daughter's.

He closed his eyes. She'd been here for mere minutes and he'd already resorted to lurking in doorways and spying. Mary's voice washed over him. "That's perfect. Just like that. Slow, even strokes."

His hands clenched into fists. Bloody hell, he wanted her to speak to him with those same words and soft tone. Just on an entirely different subject.

"Like this?" Anne asked, eager for approval. "Am I doing a good job?"

"Wonderful," Mary answered. "Your father is going to love this picnic."

He was going to love it. Every damned second.

"And then after the picnic, we can draw?"

"I'm sure we can. But first we'll have to pick the perfect thing to draw. Something that is relatively easy for our first time and something that sparks our imagination and strikes our fancy."

Sin knew what he'd draw if given the chance. He pushed the palms of his hands into his eyes. He wouldn't survive a week with Mary in the house, let alone two. He was certain of it. Stepping into the kitchen, he dropped his hands. "Anne, come get me when you're ready for the picnic."

And then, without waiting for an answer, he stomped back up the stairs to his office where he tossed himself into his chair. He had to last a week with Mary. Honestly, he had to last far longer. She was good for his daughter and he'd endured worse for the sake of Anne's happiness.

But as he tried to start working, again and again, his thoughts returned to the rich brown silk of Mary's hair and the soft shape of her eyes. The pale pink that infused her cheeks and lovely curves of her figure danced in front of his closed eyes.

He dropped his head into his hands, propping his elbows on the desk. Mary was haunting him.

CHAPTER SIX

MARY SAT ON THE BLANKET, enjoying the summer sun as she waited for Anne to return with Lord Sinclair. Here in the shade of a flowering pear tree, nothing could bother her, not even her worries over her new, temporary-for-now position.

She pulled out a sketch pad and started to draw. First, she drew a nearby daisy, dancing on the end of its stalk in the summer breeze. But her thoughts drifted to little Anne and her charcoal followed. Soon, she was adding a girl bent over and sniffing the flower.

Mary wasn't nearly as accomplished as Grace but she pictured the girl in her mind and tried to capture the child's essence. There was so much life in the girl waiting to come out. Then she thought of Lord Sinclair. Slowly, she began to sketch his outline too, behind the child, smiling in support. His hands were held out waiting to help the girl, his shoulders slightly bent in case she fell as she danced toward the flower.

It was a rough sketch, no detail added, but the subjects were clear and the picture made her smile, despite herself.

When she looked up, the real-life Anne was bounding toward her, Lord Sinclair following in her wake, just as in her drawing. Her smile broadened as she set the sketch aside and waved. Sin waved back and her grin slipped, her tongue darting out to lick her now parched lips. How could the man affect her so with the tiniest of gestures?

"Do you see, Papa? Isn't it lovely? This is so much nicer than lessons." Anne stopped just on the edge of the blanket.

Mary answered before Lord Sinclair could. "Lessons are very important too. You must be ready for life as an adult, but that doesn't mean we can't have some fun."

"Agreed," Sin said as he chose a spot across from her on the blanket. "And this picnic looks delicious. I must confess that I too wish we'd done this before now."

"Me too," Anne answered, sitting next to her father.

She reached for a bit of meat pie, but Mary held up her hand. "Remember, we serve his lordship first."

"Oh yes," Anne nodded and turned to her father. "What would you like to eat, my lord?"

Sin's eyebrows rose. "A meat pie and some chicken, please."

Mary tapped a bowl of fruit, giving Anne a wink. Anne nodded, folding her hands and turning to her father to practice her manners. "You must try the dates. They are in season and delightful."

"I will take your recommendation, my lady." And he gave Mary a long look that made her shift on the ground, her eyes dropping to her lap.

"Very good," Anne replied sitting up straighter and nodding along. "Would you also care for some tea?"

"Tea would be lovely." And then he dipped his chin in a nod of acknowledgement. Mary's breath stuck in her throat. She knew what his gesture meant. He understood what Mary had been attempting to accomplish with this picnic lunch. Anne was still engaged in lessons. The entire affair had been a big lesson on first preparing food, then learning the proper way to serve. Of course, Anne had barely noticed, which was the best way to teach someone. But Sin clearly understood what Mary was doing with the day and he appreciated her efforts.

And that was more pleasing to Mary than if he'd winked at her during a ball or asked her to dance.

They ate their meal, Anne doing her best to make the small talk as Mary had instructed her. "Isn't the day lovely?" she asked at one point.

"The breeze is a delight," Mary had answered. "And your garden, Lord Sinclair, is stunning. What a beautiful place."

Anne had clapped her hands. "Last year it was overgrown but this year we were able to hire a gardener again."

Mary didn't answer as she studied Sin. His mouth tightened as he too remained silent. She knew he'd taken over the Gaming Hell from Darlington and the others and clearly he needed the funds if he was hiring staff he hadn't previously been able to afford. Finally, she cleared her throat. "I'm so glad the gardener was able to do such a lovely job."

"Wait a moment." Anne jumped up. "There are some snapdragons I want to show you. They're my favorite flower the gardener planted this year. Maybe we'll draw those." Then the girl was off, disappearing down a path.

Mary glanced over at Sin to find his head bent low as he stared at his hands. "This picnic has been lovely. I'm glad to use the garden. I have to confess we haven't been out here much."

Mary scooted a bit closer. "I'm glad you enjoyed it. Anne certainly has and she's learning a great deal."

"I noticed," he answered. "And you're learning a great deal about us too."

Mary shook her head though he wasn't looking at her.

"My father didn't leave me with the flushest Earldom," he said still looking down. "I was struggling from the moment I took over. And after my wife passed three years ago..." His mouth turned down, as tight lines of pain marked his face.

She didn't think. Reaching out, she placed a hand on his arm. "No need to explain to me. I've lived off my aunt and uncle for the past five years. I envy you the opportunity to change your situation. I only wish that I could do the same for myself."

He placed a hand over hers and a tingling of energy spread up her arm. She looked down at the intimate gesture but then his words pulled her gaze back up. "Why don't you marry? Won't your aunt and uncle sponsor you?"

She dropped her chin to her chest. "They already financed one season. I won't be any more of a burden to them then I've already been."

"Burden?" he asked, his fingers squeezing hers. "It's your uncle's duty to care for you."

She looked at him then, his deep brown eyes drawing her in. "I suppose. I feel better, inside, when I am useful. I much prefer teaching Anne then batting my eyelashes at balls."

He stared at her for a moment longer before he leaned closer, his breath tickling her cheeks. And then, slowly, softly, he placed his lips on top of hers. She'd kissed before. But not like this. This light touch stole the air from her lungs and sent shivers of pleasure straight to her core.

Dear lord, she was in very deep trouble.

———

SIN HAD JUST MADE a terrible mistake. Mary's lush lips under his felt better than anything he'd ever experienced before. So supple and yielding, they pressed to his with a passion that belied the gentle touch.

His body responded with a roaring need. He wanted more.

Which was a mistake. He shouldn't have even kissed her. She was a tutor, his employee, and all wrong for him.

He pulled away, listening to his head even as his body protested. "Miss Chase," he growled out, his voice hoarse and deep. "My apologies. I should not have—"

Her eyes widened and her head snapped back. "Your apologies?" Then she pursed her lips. "There's no need." But she pulled her hand from his arm and used it to push herself to stand. "I'll find Anne."

Regret tightened his chest. He shouldn't have kissed her, but just as bad, he should not have expressed regret. "Wait."

She stilled, her hands fisting her skirts as though she were about to run.

"You are a very attractive woman." He stood too and reached for her hand. Reluctantly, she untangled her fingers from her skirts. He gently took her fingers in his. "But you are also under my employ and I would not want you to think I'd take advantage of that fact."

Mary's shoulders relaxed and her grip softened. "Thank you for the explanation."

"Miss Chase," Anne called. "I brought you a snapdragon in every color. Do you wish to see?"

"Very much," she answered, stepping around him to greet Anne. "Oh, they are lovely. Run to the kitchen and fetch a vase. We'll arrange them."

Anne clapped her hands. "Should I bring sheers too?"

"Yes, please, but hold them by the blade, not by the handles," she called after his daughter.

"Yes, Miss Chase," Anne called over her shoulder darting off again.

"And no running while you're holding them." Mary called as the child disappeared, leaning away from him to be heard by Anne.

He stared at her with painful awareness. She was beautiful and this first afternoon had been an oasis compared with the past several months. Did that mean she could do the job after all? And how would he cope with her living here full time? "You're going to teach her to arrange flowers?"

"I am," Mary answered, pulling her hand from his once again.

"And her fear? Is this also part of addressing that?"

Mary turned to look at him. "I first need to see what makes her afraid. Then we shall know if we can fix it." She quirked a brow at him. "So far I haven't seen anything."

He straightened, looking down at her. It was ridiculous but he had the urge to ask her if she thought she could fix him too. But of course, she couldn't. Instead, he murmured a ridiculously personal question. "She does all right most days. Better with you here. It's night that she struggles with."

She let out a long breath. "Night is difficult, isn't it? We all have fears that come out then."

"What makes you afraid?"

"My brother died as a baby. My parents in a carriage accident. My fiancé at war." She swallowed, her face tightening in pain. "I am afraid of wasting my time on this earth."

He drew in a deep breath. Her comments about working and being useful coming into focus. "Would you consider marrying to be a waste of time?"

She shook her head. "No, of course not. Having a family is the most useful thing in the world. But I can't spend years flirting in society. I won't. If that means that I spend my life helping children like Anne rather than having my own, I'm prepared for that."

"Mary," he whispered so that only she could here. Something inside him was shifting. "Such loss. And here you stand ready to help others." A great many of his doubts about her were melting away. At least the ones involving her teaching Anne.

She shook her head. "It's because of the loss, not in spite of it." Her mouth pinched. "When I lost my fiancé, Harold, usefulness was the only thing that saved me."

He grimaced, wanting to pull her close and hold her in comfort. Hell, he wanted to kiss her again.

But he couldn't do that. Even if Mary was right for Anne, she was not for him, and therefore he needed to leave her be. "I admire your strength." Her inner strength called to him, but still, how could he allow her to slip beneath his guard when he knew all too well what could happen to her delicate body during childbirth? He couldn't risk that kind of loss again. He took a step back. "I'm so glad you're here to help my daughter." He didn't bother to add that her presence was a torture for him. A sweet sort of temptation that was going to bring him to his knees.

CHAPTER SEVEN

MARY HAD a lovely afternoon sketching with Anne followed by a wonderful dinner in the nursery. Without Lord Sinclair making her tremble with attraction, her job tutoring Anne was turning out to be a delight.

Brushing out her hair, she carefully braided the long brown strands into a loose braid over her shoulder. She'd changed into a night rail and dressing gown and hummed as she worked through the hair. It had been a very satisfying day.

A cry from the other room made her sit up. The noise sounded again, louder and stronger than the first time.

Jumping from the chair, she raced into the Anne's connecting room, positive that was the noise's source.

Sure enough, the child thrashed on the bed, her cries growing louder. Mary settled next to Anne, cupping the child's cheek. "It's all right, sweetheart. You're fine."

"No," Anne whimpered, her eyes still closed. "No."

"Shhhh." Mary softly stroked the child's cheek, then she began to sing. "*Sleep my child, let peace attend thee, all through the night.*"

Anne sighed, her limbs settling back at her sides.

"*Guardian angels, God will send thee, all through the night.*"

Anne's eyes opened then. "I like that. Can you sing more?"

"*Soft the drowsy hours are keeping. In the veil of slumber sleeping. I my loving vigil keeping all through the night.*"

Anne placed her hand over Mary's. "Will you stay with me for a bit?"

"Of course," Mary answered. "There now. There's no need to worry." And she lay down on top of the covers, still stroking Anne's cheek. "I'm right here."

Anne curled into Mary's side and in seconds was back to sleep again. Mary, however, lay next to the child for a long time. Only when Anne was deeply asleep, did she finally rise from the bed and return to her room.

She didn't bother to close the door before she moved to her bed and climbed under her covers. She didn't bother to take off her dressing gown either. Mary had the feeling she'd be up again before too long. But as she relaxed into the pillow, a knock sounded at her door.

Crinkling her brow, she tossed back the cover and crossed the floor to open the large wooden panel. Sin stood on the other side, still fully dressed. Her breath caught to see him standing there in the dark. "My lord," she asked. "What is it?"

He scrubbed his face with his hands. "I heard Anne. When I went to comfort her, you were already there and I didn't think it appropriate to enter, but I wanted to check on you before I retired."

Something inside her melted a bit. He was accustomed to soothing his child back to sleep. "I'm fine and so is she." She hesitated, leaning her cheek on the edge of the door. "Do you get up with her often in the night?"

He nodded. "Three, sometimes four times. The nanny helps too, of course, but she needs a repose."

"I will see to her care this evening. You must be exhausted as well."

He gave her a sideways glance, his eyes filled with apprehension as he stepped closer. "Will you run crying from this house when the fortnight is over?"

That made her smile. "No, not because of this. But I am reconsidering the sleeping arrangements."

He took a half step closer. "How so?"

"She has a right to be afraid and she needs comfort now. I think I should sleep in the room with her until she's strong enough to be on her own."

He touched her cheek causing a shiver of pleasure to race down her spine. She nearly pulled back but he dropped his hand. "Thank you." His face spasmed in pain. "You've no idea how much I appreciate your help," he said before he turned and crossed the hall to his own room. She watched him enter and then close his door but still, she stood there, leaning against the cool wood.

He hurt too. The loss of his wife, she'd seen it earlier today. Worry for his daughter.

She closed her eyes. She could help him. Help them both. Then she thought of all she'd missed from Harold. She'd never know a man's touch, the feel of his skin against hers. Sin was lucky in one regard, his love had been complete.

Her fingers drifted to her lips as Mary remembered Sin's kiss. Nothing had prepared her for his mouth against hers.

Her conversation with Ada floated through her thoughts again. Her cousin had suggested that she marry Sin. Would he want her that way? He had kissed her but just as quickly he'd pulled away again.

Hope bubbled in her chest. For her part, she thought she might be able to help them both move past their losses and fears.

———

Sin paced his room for the better part of a quarter hour. Tired as he was, he knew there was little hope of sleep. He'd placed Anne across from his room when she'd begun having nightmares and Mary next to Anne for obvious reasons.

But now, he knew that Mary was just steps away, curled in a bed under his roof. Bloody hell, this was not going well. He shouldn't have brought her here, even provisionally.

His body tightened with an aching need as he leaned his head on the fireplace mantle, squeezing his eyes shut.

Pushing off the wood frame again, he headed for the door. Perhaps a drink in the library or a late-night walk in the garden would help him to find some sleep.

He wrenched the knob in but then stopped mid stride. Mary stood exactly where he left her, leaning against the door. "Mary?"

Her gaze, which had glassed over, snapped to his. "Oh dear. Yes. Sorry." Then she started to close the large panel.

"Wait." He stepped toward her. "Why are you still there?"

"I…" she whispered. "I was just thinking."

Desire pulsed through him. Even in the dark he saw the color fill her cheeks. "About?" he asked moving closer still. It was a dangerous game. He'd already kissed her once today.

"Marriage," she said, then sighed. "I was engaged. I know I told you already. Part of me wishes we'd married before he left. It's silly, I know. But I'd like to know what all the fuss is about."

His throat went completely dry. "Fuss?"

She shook her head, her hands fluttering up from her sides. "It doesn't matter. Late night musings. Likely had too much tea. I shall see you in the morning."

She started to close the door but he reached up and placed his hand on the edge just above her head. A single strand of her hair tickled his palm. "You want to know what the fuss is about between a man and a woman?"

She tilted her head back to look up at him, her slender neck arching toward him. "I'm not myself," she said softly. "That kiss in the garden."

He touched her cheek, letting his hands slide down her jaw and over the silken skin of her throat. "I understand completely." Then he leaned down and kissed her again. This one was not the chaste kiss of earlier, it was still soft but it burned with passion, lingering in a long, slow, burning desire. "And I think we've got a real problem."

She let out a soft sigh that was half groan and his insides flipped even as his cock went from hard to granite. "I'm going to have to leave, aren't I?"

"Perhaps," he answered, stealing another taste of her sweet nectar. "Or mayhap there is another option. Meet me in my study before breakfast. Let's say eight?"

She shook her head. "Actually, I'd prefer if you just sacked me now. I'll never sleep worrying about it."

His fingers were dancing over the base of her throat. "I am not going to sack you. If anything, your family should have me tossed in the stocks."

Her nose crinkled and it was so adorable, that he had to lean down and kiss it. "I doubt that. But if they knew of the kisses…"

"We'd be wed," he finished the thought for her. "Mary…" His voice dropped and he took a step back. "You remind me of my first wife. It's difficult—"

She parted her lips. "Oh dear," she answered. "That would be a problem."

He started to trace her collarbone. "I loved her. And when she died, part of me died too, and I'm afraid to feel that way again."

"Do you mind if I ask how we're alike? In what ways do I remind you of her?"

He swallowed, an ache burning in his throat. "She was small, slender like you. Blonde hair and classic features…" He had to stop, the words making him ache.

Her fingers reached up to cup his cheek and he found himself leaning into the touch. "I've an idea," she said moving closer. "What if we simply engage in a marriage of convenience? I can help you raise Anne. Give you the heir you still need—"

"Mary," he warned. "I'm not sure I can give you what you deserve. My heart is half gone already." And if she were to become pregnant… he'd perish with worry.

She raised her brows. "As is mine."

His shoulders slumped. That was a good point. "I won't be able to love you."

She shook her head. "I'm not asking for your love. I just want a future of my own. In the process, I will aid you with yours."

"A marriage of convenience?" He leaned down again, stealing another kiss and then another. "The idea has merit."

He slid his hand down her arm, then laced her fingers through his. "I could be here for you and for Anne," she said.

His eyebrows rose. "And I could make you a countess. A far better life than that of a tutor."

She stepped back then, adding space between them. "Eight tomorrow?"

"Tomorrow," he answered. But he didn't want to wait. He wanted to touch her right now. Which might really be an issue with a marriage of convenience.

CHAPTER EIGHT

MARY ENDED up sleeping in Anne's bed. The child was so afraid and they both got far more sleep that way. Still as she made her way down the stairs the next morning, she wondered if her exhaustion was going to impact her ability to reason with Sin.

Pausing just outside his office, Mary pinched her cheeks. If she were honest, even when Anne was sleeping, she'd been awake thinking about the lord across the hall. Her Chase heritage had reared its head again as she'd actually managed to propose to an earl.

She pushed her fingertips into the sockets of her eyes. Ridiculous. At least he seemed to be considering the proposal.

Which was what had caused the sleeplessness. Every time she thought about actually being married to the man… visions of his kisses, the way he touched her danced through her thoughts.

Then there were the other possibilities. Like bearing a baby of her own. She'd thought those possibilities had died with Harold and it had taken her a long time to open herself to them again. Which was why she needed to be gentle with Sin now.

Dropping her hands, she pinched her cheeks again. Mentally, she worked through her list of rational reasons why this marriage was a smart decision on his part.

"Mary," he called from in the office. "Are you going to come in?"

Everything inside her went rigid, making it difficult to move. "Perhaps. I just need a few more minutes in the hall."

He chuckled and she relaxed at the sound. "Why don't you come in here and think your thoughts. I've got a pot of tea waiting for you."

Her shoulders slumped as a small smile graced her lips. "You understand me already."

"Perhaps a little," he answered.

She entered the room to find him standing by the window, his gaze focused on the ground below. She glanced out to see the garden and the spot in which they'd picnicked the day before. "Did you sleep at all last night?"

"Not much," he answered. "I'll try to rest this afternoon. Tonight, I am off to the club."

She supposed she'd sleep better knowing he wasn't in the house but a part of her was disappointed too. Mary liked being near him. "What are those clubs like?"

He looked up at her then. "They are dark and rather…" He paused. "A lot of men doing a lot of drinking and a fair bit of fighting because money and liquor are involved."

"Sounds lovely." She stepped up to the tray of tea. "Would you like a cup?"

He turned to her then, his eyes drinking her in. "It is a necessity to make sure that Anne is provided for." Then he hesitated. "And my future heir, of course. He must inherit a sustainable earldom." Why did he grimace when he mentioned another child?

She held her breath. "You've considered my offer."

He took the cup of tea she offered, his fingers brushing hers. "I have."

She picked up her own cup and brought it to her lips, trying to hide the tremble. As an earl he had lots of options as to who he took for a bride, but for her, this might be her last chance to marry. Taking a sip, she then clamped her teeth together to keep from commenting.

"I lost my first wife during the birthing of my second child." He

46

turned to the window again. "He was a boy, but he didn't survive either."

So he'd suffered two losses, not one. And a life so small and fragile. No wonder he was so hesitant. "I'm sorry."

He looked back at her. "My hesitation is not that you're unsuitable in any way but you're so small." His gaze raked up and down her. "I worry that I'll lose you too."

The cup nearly slipped from her fingers as tears filled her eyes. "I won't make you a false promise. Life is so uncertain, I can attest to that more than anyone. But even strong, healthy people die. It is part of life, I'm afraid." But honestly, she wasn't that worried. She didn't wish to belittle his fears but she'd always been healthy, strong. And the women in her family birthed children exceptionally well. "But of the things that I worry about, childbirth isn't one of them. A life without meaning, however, scares me to no end."

He nodded, relaxing a bit. "I appreciate your perspective and I'm glad you're not afraid. I'm a large man though, and I seem to create large babies and—" He scrubbed his hands over his face.

She set down the cup and placed a hand on his shoulder, her own heart aching. "I understand. I can't imagine how I'd feel if I thought you were going off to war."

He looked up at her then. "You do understand. Which is why I've decided to marry if you you'll accept my terms."

She dropped her hand as her stomach started to churn with dread. "Terms?"

He swallowed, his Adam's apple bobbing. "You've already agreed to help me raise Anne. I've every confidence you'll make a good stepmother."

That eased the ache a bit. "Of course."

"But I only wish to have one more child." He didn't look at her, his expression shuddered and drawn tight.

Her brows drew together. "But what if it's another girl?"

He shrugged. "We'll figure that out if it comes to pass. But I won't risk more."

She shook her head. He wasn't making sense. Bearing one child was as risky as having a second one and, as she'd already stated, the entire point was to have a boy. Besides, other women built like her had babies all the time. Surely, there was another reason for his wife's devastating death. She didn't broach the subject now. After all, he'd given her an opportunity to get married and start her own family, have her own life.

For now, this was the closest to a happily ever after she'd likely get. "I consent to the terms." She'd figure out how to get him to move past his grief and false beliefs after they said their vows.

———

SIN NEARLY SLUMPED FORWARD in relief but held himself up. The truth of the matter was that he wanted Mary, desperately so. But of course, for her sake and for his, he couldn't have her bear many children.

If he could avoid getting her pregnant all together, he would. But he felt compelled to give it one more try for the sake of the title and his duty. After that, he'd cease his physical relationship with her and focus on just being a good father and husband.

He ignored the cry of protest his body made. Impregnating her once was all the risk he could take. He shouldn't even do that.

She tentatively slid her fingers into his. "If it makes you feel better, my mother bore two children and suffered no ill effects. I'm slightly taller than she was."

He looked up at her, unable to hide his surprise. "You have a sibling?"

She shook her head. "Disease of the lung when he was just three."

He made a soft sound that rumbled in his throat and echoed about the room. "You lost your entire family." Without thought, he pulled her into his arms tucking her head under his chin. She melted into him her chest pressing to his rib cage, her softness so right against his muscles. "It's all right," he whispered, starting to stroke her back. "I understand."

"We do understand each other, don't we?" she said into his neck, her voice vibrating through him.

He leaned down and softly kissed the top of her head. "We do. I must confess that it's one of the many reasons I accepted your proposal."

She winced, he felt the tightening of her facial muscles. "I still can't believe I did that."

Squeezing her tighter for a moment, he loosened his grip and leaned back to look down into those beautiful blue eyes. "I'm glad you did."

"Really?" she asked, her eyes crinkling at the corners.

How did he explain, without sounding weak, that it might have taken him weeks to draw the conclusions she'd forced? That grief had held him in its grip and he'd only just started to rise from its ashes. "Really." He bent down and kissed her nose again. It was an adorable nose and he rather enjoyed giving it small kisses. "Now tell me. How did the night go with Anne?"

Mary frowned. "You were right. That is her struggle. I have to find a way to break her cycle of fear. Not sure what it is yet but I do know that until then, there is little point in fighting her feelings. She's frightened and what she needs is support and to slowly build her own self value."

His hand came to cup her cheek. "Thank you." He fought the urge to kiss her again. Somehow, her work with Anne only made him want her that much more. "You've no idea what this means to me."

She gave a nod, looking up at him. "If we're successful, I will someday."

His hand slipped from her face. That was true. And it made him cold to think about. Was it wrong to hope that she never actually became pregnant? "True." Gently he moved her back, slipping away from the window to cross from the desk. "I'll go see your uncle today to ask for your hand."

"I'm sure he'll consent," she answered. "They've been on me for years to join society again."

He quirked a brow. "You've been in my house for a day. He's likely to think I'm a terrible ogre who hurt you in some fashion."

Her eyebrows rose up as her lips pressed together. "Perhaps Anne and I should make the trip with you. Not only will they see that I am absolutely fine but then Anne can see Grace's studio." She picked up her tea. "Besides, you need only tell my uncle that I asked you and he'll understand. He's aware of Chase women's tendencies." She frowned, her features growing tight.

"I'd love it if you both came with and thank you for the advice." He rubbed his chin as he considered her. This was not the first time she'd lamented her Chase heritage. "We'll leave in two hours if that's amenable to you?"

"Of course," she answered, setting down her cup. "I'll go up and begin getting Anne ready."

"Excellent." He watched as she headed for the door and then left, the sway of her hips dancing before his eyes long after she'd disappeared. It was very possible that he'd just entered a bargain with the devil. Because while Mary was an angel, what she did to his body was sin at its finest and he didn't know how he was going to find the strength to resist.

The contract they'd entered required control, the very thing, when it came to her, he did not have.

CHAPTER NINE

MARY HELD the wood rail in the carriage, determined not to watch Sin's every move. His thighs flexed as he shifted his legs, his breeches making every muscle's delightful ripple known to her.

An ache throbbed between her legs and held in her breath, trying to calm her racing heart.

"Are we going to see your cousin who's a painter?" Anne asked, reaching for Mary's hand.

"I don't think so," she answered and the girl made a loud groan. She gently squeezed the child's hand. "Patience," she softly whispered. "If you're good we can go into her studio and try out some of her paints on canvas."

Anne let out a gasp of delight and Sin chuckled appreciatively. The sound of his deep baritone trilled up and down her spine.

"Papa, are you going to paint with us too?" Anne bounced on her seat.

Sin shook his head. "No, my sweet. I'm going to speak with Mary's uncle."

Anne stopped bouncing to cock her head. "Why do you need to speak with him?"

Sin gave her a wink. "Be a good girl like Mary said and we'll discuss it this evening."

The rest of the ride passed in lovely chatter with Mary sneaking glances at Sin as her blood heated.

When they finally arrived, she wished she could be like Anne and rocket out of the carriage. Energy and heat flowed through her and Mary desperately needed some fresh air to cool her skin.

Sin helped her from the carriage, his hand lingering on hers before he tucked it into his elbow and then they made their way up the steps.

Her aunt and uncle greeted them as soon as they walked through the foyer. Mary stopped in surprise. "Are you expecting someone?"

"Yes." Her aunt raised her brows. "You."

Mary looked over at Sin. But before she could ask, her uncle answered.

"Lord Sinclair sent a missive you were coming."

"Did we miss anything?" Minnie called from behind her and Mary turned with a gasp. Several carriages were pulling up the drive. Minnie and Daring stood just behind her while Malice and Cordelia came up the front walk.

"Miss anything?" Mary asked, turning back to her aunt. "What is everyone doing here?"

Her uncle stepped forward. "We're making sure that everything is happening the proper way."

Mary's mouth fell open. She knew what this meant. Her uncle wanted his sons-in-law in attendance in case Sin hadn't behaved himself. "This was not necessary. Lord Sinclair and I—"

"I will be the judge of what's necessary," her uncle replied.

Mary's face heated even as her shoulders snapped back and her chin raised. "You are not to make this more difficult than it needs to be. Am I clear?"

Her uncle's eyes widened, but Daring chuckled behind them. "Mary, you're more like Minnie than I first imagined."

That made Mary deflate. Her personality was rearing its ugly head again. "My apologies, Uncle."

Her uncle assessed her for a moment. "Do not apologize to me child. I raised you to be this way."

She swallowed, her shoulders hunching. "Why would you inflict this curse upon us?"

"Curse?" Minnie asked.

"What curse?" Malice asked from the back, having reached the group. "Did a gypsy curse us? Is that why we all keep getting married? Did anyone warn Sin before he took over the club?"

Daring spun back around. "A gypsy has certainly cursed your tongue. It never flaps that much."

Vice laughed having reached the steps. "Is Malice talking? Marriage does agree with him."

Sin cleared his throat. "No one needs to warn me of anything. I've been searching for a bride for some time. I may as well state my intentions now. When Mary happened upon my door—though I suspect Daring planned it all along and he is our gypsy—I rather quickly decided not to squander the opportunity. I'm here to formally ask for her hand. That is all."

Her uncle opened his mouth to speak, but Anne interrupted. "Is that the surprise?" Then she let go of Mary's hand, clapping and jumping in the air. "Miss Chase is to be my new mother." And she launched herself at Mary, who caught the child in a hug.

Sin patted his daughter's back. "If anyone questions my reasons, I would like to refer them to my daughter's excitement."

A laugh broke out among the group as everyone relaxed, including her uncle. "Well, apologies for bringing everyone here this morning. But since you've all come, let's have lunch, shall we?"

Applause broke out.

Mary buried her nose in Anne's hair, hiding her face. While Sin had handled the situation well, part of her cringed that Anne was the reason he wanted to marry her. She knew that this was a marriage of convenience but some small part of her wanted him to want more.

Her uncle reached out to shake Sin's hand. "Let's discuss the details while the women catch up."

Mary lifted her head, a frown marking her face. She'd expected to face her aunt, but her cousins? Would they understand the bargain she'd just made?

————

SIN ASSESSED the ring of men around him trying to process what he'd just learned. In addition to Mary's uncle, Lord Winthorpe, Daring, Malice, Exile, Bad, and Vice all sat around him. They had collectively come together to provide Mary with the dowry she'd never had from her family.

"So you've raised a dowry for her? But she already has a proposal?"

Daring shrugged. "We didn't know that, of course. We hoped to increase her chances of a proposal by making her wealthier."

Sin gave his head a slow shake. "So now that's engaged..."

"The dowry is yours." Vice winked at him. "Our mission was accomplished. She's received an offer from a titled lord, no less."

"Did you think to tempt me with the carrot of wealth?" He leaned forward his elbows braced on his knees.

Malice shrugged. "You were one of the men we were considering."

At the thought of other men, he shot up straight. "Who else?"

"It doesn't matter now," Bad answered, his brows low and heavy over his eyes. "You've offered."

"And even better, it wasn't for money." Exile leaned back in his chair one foot propped on the other knee.

"What is the reason?" Vice asked. "Have you fallen in love?"

"No," he answered rather too quickly than necessary. "She is lovely, which helps." He didn't care to admit how much he was looking forward to bedding Mary. "And she is wonderful with my daughter. That is the basis of my decision."

Vice snorted. A loud, obvious sound that echoed in the room full of men. "Liar."

Daring gave a light chuckle. "Let the man delude himself if he must."

Sin's lips thinned, stretching over his teeth. "My feelings are my own and none of your concern. I know that each of you is newly in

54

love but I was you once. And then my wife died while birthing my son."

Their mirth died. Vice lost the devilish twinkle, while Daring's mouth pulled down. Exile straightened, and Lord Winthorpe shifted in his seat. "Loss is difficult to bear. Are you certain you're ready to marry again?"

Sin looked down at his hands. What Winthorpe actually meant was, *are you whole enough for my niece?* "Mary and I both understand loss. It makes it easier to marry again knowing that she has suffered as I have. She's learned to bear the weight of losing her fiancé, her parents, and brother. I can only hope she'll teach me to be as strong." The words echoed about his thoughts. Hellfire and damnation. The words rang in his head.

All this time he'd been too worried about Mary being weak. But she was the stronger of the two of them. And she, after one day, had pulled him further out of his emotional hole than anyone else he'd ever met.

"That was very well said." Bad clapped him on the shoulder. "Whether it's love or just admiration, I'd say the two of you are well-suited." Then he cleared his throat. "I grew up on the streets, not even a roof over my head. I thought…" Bad hesitated. "I thought I didn't deserve love. But when you let the right woman in, she makes you better."

Sin stared at Bad. "For a man who rarely speaks, you're very articulate." He scrubbed his face as Bad's words sunk in. Did Sin think he didn't deserve love? He drew in a shuddering breath. The answer was yes.

CHAPTER TEN

FACING a room of Chase women was a lot like what Mary imagined standing against an army might feel like. Cold sweat covered her palms, and she stood poised ready to run.

Minnie, the oldest of the all the girls, the first to marry, a duke no less, and the most outspoken stepped forward first, her red hair glinting in the sun. "You're engaged?"

Mary tucked her hands in her skirt, covertly wiping away the sweat. "Yes. It would seem so." She knew once the details of the arrangement became known, her family would have a great deal to say.

Diana slowly rose from her chair. "It's impressive that you were able to gain an offer in a single day. Not that I didn't have faith in you. But still."

She swallowed. Did she admit he hadn't asked her? "He was already looking for a wife."

Cordelia pushed up her glasses. "I find that concerning. Mary deserves more than to be a bride of convenience."

Mary gripped her skirts. "You're wrong. I am lucky to have this chance at all."

Grace brushed an invisible strand of blonde hair back from her lovely face. "What are you talking about? You're beautiful, kind, and strong. You deserve the very best."

Mary shook her head. They didn't understand. "My chance at love died five years ago. I wasted it away…"

"What does that mean?" Minnie asked.

Mary sat in the chair behind her. "I was so angry that Harold wished to go on another military tour. Instead of asking him kindly or with love, I railed at him in anger. I practically pushed him out the door. He died a month later. My Chase temper, it—"

"You don't really believe that?" Diana pushed out of her chair and crossed the room, crouching before Mary. "If he'd had a choice, he would have returned for you. You can't blame yourself."

Mary shook her head. "I must be to blame. My father, mother, brother, and fiancé are all gone. I try to do good in this world, but I must have done something terribly wrong to—" She couldn't finish, a sob breaking free from her chest.

Diana wrapped her in a hug, Minnie joining until Cordelia and Grace had wrapped her up too. "You didn't do anything wrong," Cordelia said, squeezing the whole group. "Life has been cruel to you. You, however, have done an admirable job of rising above that. And it's your turn for happiness. Don't forget that."

Tears spilled down her cheeks. How did she explain that Sin made her happy? Perhaps it wasn't what they had. She'd just met him, but the idea of what they could build together filled her with joy. Though in her heart of hearts she wished for love, she was content to be a wife and a mother, and she'd make the most of this situation. "Thank you for saying that. I suppose it's time that I confess to you he didn't ask me to marry him."

The hug loosened as her cousins stepped back forming a ring about her chair. "What does that mean?" Minnie asked.

But Diana let out a peal of laughter. "You asked him."

Mary nodded. "My Chase sensibilities took over." She twisted her hands in her lap. "I find him to be…"

"Gorgeous," Grace suggested.

"Stunning," Diana corrected.

Minnie tapped her chin. "Handsome as Sin."

They all laughed. "And he hurts too. He needs someone to—"

"Oh dear lord," Cordelia gasped. "Not only are you trying to save Anne but you're going to help him recover from his grief." She reached for Mary's hand. "How can you not see how good you are?"

Diana pressed a hand to her shoulder. "And be careful. A man like that… It would be so easy for you to end up hurt."

Mary winced, her mouth twisting into a frown. Diana was right. Her feelings were already involved. "He is attracted to me, I know that."

Grace nodded. "That attraction could turn to love."

No one spoke for a moment. "How though?" Diana asked the room in general. "What forces a man to develop such feelings."

Cordelia tapped her chin. "Well, for us, there was an element of danger involved. They were saving us. Mary doesn't have the threat of real violence hanging over her head but…"

Grace spread her hands in front of her. "What if we fabricated it?"

"What?" Mary asked, her stomach twisting. She didn't like where this was going. "I don't think…"

"She could fall into the Thames," Grace raised a finger. "Or be in danger of a runaway carriage."

Diana gasped and Mary was certain her cousin would put a stop to this madness. "Or we could have one of our husbands attempt to kidnap her so Sin would have to save her."

"You've lost your senses," she said. "We're not tricking him in any way. It's a terrible idea. After what he's been through—"

"I think it has merit," Diana sniffed, her dark hair glinting in the sun.

"That's enough," Minnie said from just behind Mary. "We'll trust Mary to find her own way." She leaned down and kissed Mary's cheek. "But ask us for help, would you? You've done so much for us, don't be afraid to ask us to return the favor."

Mary nibbled her lip. In this, there wasn't much they could do to help. Mary had gone and fallen in love with a man who didn't love her back. Was there anything she could do for herself?

———

SIN SAT at his desk watching the sun sink below the buildings in the distance. He'd spent the afternoon mired in reports from his land and the business, which had been a welcome distraction from his thoughts of the blonde-haired beauty flitting about his home.

He'd caught scraps of sound from Anne and Mary as they moved about the house. A laugh here, a crash there. Each one pulled at his legs, making his feet itch to find the two most important women in his life. He loved Anne with all his heart but he was beginning to think that Mary might claim it as well.

Which stole his breath. He pushed back from the desk, banging the chair into the wall behind. What was happening to him?

"Sin?" a feminine voice called from the other side of the door.

Mary. He skirted around the desk, crossing the room in a couple large strides. He yanked open the door to find her standing on the other side with her fist raised to knock.

He reached for her hand and pulled her into the room, closing the door behind her. After the path his thoughts had travelled, somehow holding her in his arms seemed the perfect solution to his fear over his feelings. "Don't call me that." And then he gathered her into his arms crushing her against his chest.

"What should I call you then?" She placed her hands on his shoulders.

He raised a brow as her body fit against his. He drew in a deep breath, breathing in her scent. She smelled of vanilla and wildflowers. Without thinking, he dropped his nose into her neck, surrounding himself with her. "Call me Cole," he said. "It seems far more fitting for my wife than Sin."

Her lips grazed his shoulder, soft and tender. "Cole," she repeated. Then again. "Cole." The second one came out as almost a sigh.

He loved the sound more than he could express with words. It shivered down his spine, settling in his groin and tightening both his chest and his cock. "The way you say my name. It makes me want you so much. I—"

Her lips travelled to his neck. "Cole," she murmured against his skin, so the vibration of her voice echoed down into his soul.

Pulling back, he turned his head to capture those lips with his own. It was a simple kiss, the joining of two pairs of lips, but somehow, it was so much more. The touch spoke of feelings no words could. His passion for her, his growing conviction that he loved her, but also, under that, his fear. What if something happened to her? "Mary. We're not married yet. I…" He didn't know how to say that since Clara's death, he hadn't been with another woman. The intimacy had been more than he could bear.

She skimmed her hands across his shoulders in a light touch. "I've never been with a man." She kissed him then. "We don't have to do any of that today."

He straightened, looking down into the exquisite palette of her face, the ache inside him intensifying. Inwardly, however, he berated himself. She'd loved and lost too, and she needed something from him now. The way she touched him, the way she'd sighed out his name. This wasn't just about him. "What is it you would like to do?"

Her lip trembled as it parted. "I just came to check on you. I know my family can be rough. And then…" She drew in a breath searching his eyes.

"Then?" he asked.

She gripped his shoulders tighter. "I've never experienced any passion at all really. I just…"

Sin understood. And he knew just what to do.

CHAPTER ELEVEN

MARY THOUGHT she might be going to hell for her wanton behavior. Never mind her thoughts. Those were naughty.

But Cole had tucked her against him, the hard feel of his body making her insides turn to jelly. Even more exciting was the stiff man parts pressing into her much softer belly. She ached with desire to know more, to experience the passion he effortlessly brought out in her.

He brushed his thumb across her lips and then he dropped his mouth to hers again. This kiss ignited the fire inside her as he slanted her lips open and brushed his tongue against hers. She held tight to his shoulders, her knees threatening to buckle.

But, apparently, he wasn't done with her. A thick carpet lay under their feet. With his hands tight about her waist, he guided her back until they were both on the floor, her on the carpet and him perched above her, his mouth still locked with hers.

Then his hands began skimming down her body. He cupped her breasts, tweaking her nipples before he moved lower across the flat of her stomach, around her hip and down her leg. She wore a light muslin gown, with the weather so warm, and very little underneath so that when his fingers grasped her hem, he was able to easily lift her skirts. Her pantaloons were rather sheer and his fingers skimming along the fabric were almost like he was touching her skin and goosebumps broke out all along her flesh.

He slid his lips across her jaw and down her chin. "I can't wait to see you in my bed," he whispered close to her ear. "I'm going to strip off every stitch of clothing and kiss every inch of your skin."

Heat, warmth, and wetness was flooding between her thighs and, as if he sensed that, his hand sought out the area. Finding the slit in her pantaloons, he trailed his fingers through her curls and then gently along the slit of her womanhood, causing her to let out a gasping moan. He smiled against her neck. "Do you like that?"

"Yes," she didn't hesitate in her answer. "Oh yes." She still gripped his shoulders and she started kneading the skin in her restless want of more.

He brushed the flesh again and again, her head beginning to toss from side to side until he finally parted her soft folds and slid his middle finger through them again. Her hips bucked and she said his name again. "Cole." It was a plea, a cry for more, the neediness coming through in the high pitch of her voice.

"Yes?" he chuckled, caressing his hand up and down again until he found her opening and suddenly, slid a finger inside her channel.

She gasped in a breath, feeling both needier and more complete all in the same breath. As the heel of his hand pressed against her sensitive nub, she rocked against him. "Oh," she moaned. "Cole."

"Say my name again," he spoke against her neck. "Say it over and over and I'll give you everything you want."

She blinked her eyes open. "Everything?" Hope filled her chest, making her lighter. Would he give her his heart?

"Everything, love," he answered, pulling out and pushing back into her.

She closed her eyes again. In this moment, she would pretend. Pretend that it meant something he'd used the word love. Make believe that he'd meant his heart as well as physical pleasure. "Yes," she hissed. "I want everything."

HER WORDS nearly undid his last shred of control. He wanted everything too. He wanted to bury his cock deep inside her. He wanted to hear her moan his name in pleasure when he did. But mostly, he wanted to tuck her against him and keep her there, warm and safe forever. And that was the problem.

No matter what he did, there were no guarantees in life. She could be gone in an instant…ripped from his arms.

That thought was the only one that kept him sane. Insured that he didn't undo the stays of his breeches and take her right here in the office.

Instead, he pushed his finger in deeper, taking pleasure from her reactions, her moans and cries of pleasure as he watched those lovely lips part. Her eyes dilated, her cheeks flushed, and her body writhed in tandem with his strokes inside her.

And when she came undone, she cried his name again, her neck arching. He kissed the slender column, his own body begging for more. Instead, he gently pulled his finger from inside her, closing her pantaloons, and pulling down her skirt. "How was that for your first experience?"

Her eyes, which had drifted closed, fluttered open and a sassy little smile played upon her lips. "What I am wondering is if that's as good as it gets or if it gets better?"

He nearly spilled his seed in his pants. "Mary," he pushed out between gritted teeth. "Do you want to make it to our wedding a virgin?"

Her eyes closed again. "Not particularly." Then she skimmed her hand down his back until it reached his ass. She gave his cheek a light squeeze. "Do you want me to?"

He throbbed. "No and yes."

She stiffened underneath him. Stiffened away. "What does that mean?"

Did he tell her that he was afraid to be with a woman again? That such intimacy frightened him after his loss? "I did promise your family there was nothing untoward happening."

She relaxed again. "And there wasn't. Now we're engaged."

She did have a point. And the part that wanted to be inside her was slowly but surely overruling his worries. "What if you get pregnant before the wedding?" Or at all.

She sighed again and he realized that he loved her little sounds. "We'll have a baby that much sooner."

He pulled back. "Is that a good thing?" He knew they'd discussed an heir but the more he considered the idea, the riskier it seemed.

She cupped his cheeks with her hands. "Does it make you feel better to know that the women in my family have very few problems with birthing?"

That did actually. A lot. Air rushed from his chest. "Even the small ones?"

She gave him a grin. "Even the small ones. We're a tenacious bunch."

He lifted her skirt again. This was less of the seductive caress and more of a needy yank. "And you're sure you don't want to wait until our wedding?" His grip on control was slipping away.

"I'm sure," she said quietly next to his ear. "I've been waiting since forever."

He fumbled with the fall of his breeches even as he peppered her neck with kisses. "Mary. It's been so long I..." Did he want to tell her he couldn't control himself? He took several deep breaths as he parted her pantaloons again, the silky fabric brushing against his thighs.

She slid her fingers into his hair, pulling him tighter to his chest. "I'm ready for you."

His entire body responding to those words, hardening, lengthening. As beautiful as he found her, her voice might be the most erotic feature of them all and it undid his control as he pressed the head of his cock against her soft folds. She was so wet and ready that he slid inside her without much resistance, her tight channel wrapping him in warmth. A low groan slid from his throat, as he stopped, not wanting to hurt her. But her arms tightened, encouraging him to keep going so he tilted his hips closer to hers, pushing further inside.

She made a small whimper but he froze nonetheless, lifting his head to look into her face. "Mary."

A thin smiled graced her lips. "I'm all right. I knew it would hurt the first time. Keep going."

"Are you sure?" he asked, searching her face.

Her smile grew. "The benefit of age. A little pain never hurt anyone." Then she leaned up and kissed him. "I want to be yours, Cole. All yours."

Her lips, her voice uttering those words, unseated the last of his reserve. He thrust fully inside her, her maidenhead giving way. "It's done," he gritted out, even as she locked her arms about his neck and buried her face in his shoulder.

She let out a little gasping breath that sounded half like a laugh. "I never thought this day would come." Then she gave his back a little tap with her hand. "Keep going. What's next?"

He shook his head but slowly moved out and then back inside her. Starting a rhythm, she relaxed underneath him. A minute or two passed and his own control grew thin. "I'm not sure I can last much, it's been so long."

"Don't last then." She kissed the lobe of his ear. "Cole."

Her whispering his name was his final undoing. In a roar, he finished, his seed spilling inside her. But something else, deep in his chest, came undone as well. A flood of feelings he'd been holding back for ages poured out from inside. There was love. He was falling in love with this woman, he couldn't deny it any longer. There was hope too.

But there was also grief and fear. Sharp, it bit behind his eyes making them sting with unshed tears. He was opening himself up again and that was bloody frightening.

CHAPTER TWELVE

MARY GAVE Cole another squeeze about his shoulders. She wasn't certain if he was awake or asleep but his weight had collapsed on top of hers. She liked it, immensely, but it was getting difficult to breathe. "Cole," she placed a kiss where his shoulder met his neck.

"Mmmh," he answered, not really moving.

"Are you awake?" she asked stroking his back.

"Mmmh."

She moved under him wondering if she could wriggle to the side to get more air. She didn't want to disrupt the moment, it was one of the best in her life, she just didn't want to faint during it either.

"Mary," he said, lifting his head. "If you keep moving like that, we're going to have to do it again and I don't think your body's ready for more."

She tried to giggle but it came out as a gasping breath. "It's just that you're squishing me," she finally admitted. "You're quite a bit larger than I am."

His face shuddered and he immediately rolled to the side. "I shouldn't have done that."

Mary scrunched her brow. This close, she could feel the tension reenter his body. "Squish me?" she asked as he started to pull further away but her arms were still about his neck and she held on tight, moving with him as he came to his side. She touched her nose to his. "Tell me what I've done to upset you."

"I'm not—"

"You are." She touched her forehead to his. "This close you can't lie to me. I feel your change."

He slumped then, gathering her close. "My first wife was a small woman. I loved protecting her until I couldn't."

Mary's heart thudded in her chest and she understood the full extent of his fear. In this way, she was the worst choice for his wife. She squeezed him tight to her chest. "Tell me how me and your wife are different."

He drew in a deep breath. "She'd been sickly as a child. She'd outgrown the disease but…"

She smiled, rubbing her nose softly against his. "Does it help you at all to know that I never get sick? I rarely even have colds. Even when I tended my cousins as children."

His eyes brightened. "It does."

"How was her first delivery with Anne?"

"Awful." He shuddered again, then he locked his gaze on hers. "You said your family delivers babies with ease?"

Anne nodded. "I don't want to make you false promises. But I can tell you, for better or for worse, often for worse, I am rather strong of character and body too."

"I love that about you." And then he captured her mouth in a searing kiss.

For her part, she closed her eyes and pretended he'd just said, I love you. And in her heart, she said the words back. She knew he'd put an end date on their physical relationship but for her, she didn't want that part to end. Perhaps if the baby was born with ease, he'd change his mind?

She did want to laugh with joy that her Chase tenacity, the very thing she'd hated about herself, was the one thing he loved. Could she win his heart with strength alone? She knew she had to try.

———

SIN CAREFULLY STRAIGHTENED Mary's clothing. He'd like to take her directly to his bed and keep her there for the entire night but Anne needed Mary more than he did. Still, some part of him cried out to keep her close. It wasn't just Anne whom Mary was mending. He also felt the changes happening inside his heart, his soul.

"I'll join you and Anne in the nursery for dinner," he whispered close to her ear. He ran his fingers from her neck to her shoulder.

She reached up and touched his cheek. "I'd like that." Standing on tiptoe, she pressed a kiss to his mouth. "Thank you for everything."

"Everything?" His heart battered his rib cage, it beat so fast.

"For accepting my proposal, for this…" She gestured toward the carpet as she licked her lips. "Even if I were to die an early death." She gripped his hands. "This time with you has made my life complete. I would die happy and—" Her breath caught. "I'm afraid I've quite fallen in love with you." Then she released his hand and spun toward the door. But as the heavy panel swung open, she stopped short.

Reeves stood in the doorway, his face scrunched in pain as he stared at Sin. "You've allowed a viper into our midst."

Sin sucked in his breath as Mary took a step back. He wrapped an arm about her waist and pulled her back to his chest. "You overstep."

Reeves sneered. "I'm protecting you. You can't see that this woman is using her beauty to manipulate you into gaining the position of mistress. One she does not belong in."

Mary let out a gasp, covering her mouth with her hands, a shudder running through her body. Sin carefully tucked her behind him, stepping toward Reeves. "You will be making the trip to my country estate first thing in the morning. You will stay there until I decide what to do with you."

"But, my lord." Reeve's brows drew together. "I am protecting you. She's…" he pointed to Mary, "a social climber."

Mary's hand slid to Sin's shoulder. "Reeves," she spoke softly. "Your commitment to your lord's happiness is commendable."

Sin shook his head. "And your opinion of my fiancée is misplaced. Mary's uncle is an earl."

Reeves let out a soft whoosh of breath. "I didn't know. Besides..." He held up his hands. "She's small like Lady Sinclair. What if-—"

"Enough," Sin cut the other man off. Reeves had been the family's butler since he'd been a boy of ten. With his grief and without a mistress, he'd allowed Reeves to take over many tasks, but he was beginning to understand that he'd allowed a lot of life to slip out of his control, including his own fears. "Reeves, you've been a faithful employee and I am most grateful. But my marriage is none of your concern. If you value your position here, you will turn around and go to your room and pack your bag at once."

Reeves' face fell. "I only want what's best for you."

"Don't sack him," Mary whispered low so only he could hear.

He turned back to drink in her lovely features still flushed from their lovemaking. "He was rude to you."

"He'll learn his place." Mary looked over his shoulder at Reeves. "Loyalty is a difficult trait to find."

Sin shook his head. "You are unfailingly the kindest person I've ever met." He looked back at Reeves. "Perhaps you would like to edit your opinion of the new mistress of the house?"

Reeves eyes grew very round. "It's been decided then?" The man took a half step back. "You'll marry her."

Sin pointed his finger toward the door. Mary was likely right that Reeves' loyalty was unfailing but he couldn't have Reeves pestering his new bride either. Mary needed time and space to put this family back together. And he was ready to help her in that mission. "You'll spend the summer in the country. I hope you'll use your trip for reflection. When we join you in the fall, you'll greet the new countess with all the respect her title deserves."

Reeves gave a quick jerk of his chin. "Yes, my lord." Then he spun about and raced down the hall.

After he left, Sin turned to Mary, wrapping his arms about her. "Are you all right?"

She nodded but didn't meet his eye. "Fine."

He placed a hand under her chin. "You can't lie to me when we're this close. I can feel it."

That brought a ghost of a smile to her lips. "It's just that when you said my size made you afraid, I thought you were too close to the situation to see it for what it was. But when Reeves said it..." She shook her head. "I did coerce you into proposing. Reeves is right about that. What if I'm leading you down the wrong path?"

If he thought he'd loved this woman before, he nearly burst with the emotion now. "Reeves is overstepping and the reason for that is me. I've needed someone to take me by the hand and show me the way. I allowed his role in this house to grow beyond what it should be because I wasn't able..." He paused. "Mary, no other woman could have brought me so far in so little time. You are not a temptation to be denied. More and more, I think you're my redemption."

CHAPTER THIRTEEN

COLE'S WORDS filled her with hope. A feeling that carried her through the night and into the next morning. From that hope, grew joy when she learned they'd be wed within a fortnight. Her uncle had been able to secure the license for their nuptials.

So when Anne, bounding with enthusiasm, asked if they could celebrate with a picnic in the park, Mary agreed. The child had slept fitfully with Mary in the bed across the room and all around, it seemed like a day for celebration.

Cole had gone out for the morning, but she left a note on his desk, that they'd journeyed to the nearby park with a picnic lunch. She invited him to join them if he was able.

Setting out, they made their way to a perfect picnic spot next to a large pond with several rowboats parked on a pier. Anne clapped with delight. "Can we take one for a row?"

Mary smiled as she turned back to the basket. "In a bit. First let's get our picnic set up." Much of London would journey out to walk or ride in parks such as these, but many would wait until the afternoon. It was still early yet and only a few others graced the paths at this time of the morning. "We'll set up in the shade of that tree so that we might spend the day if we'd like. I brought some paint supplies and—" She stopped as she heard the scrape of wood against wood.

Anne had traversed the dock and was pushing off the pier in her little boat. "Anne," Mary called sharply. "Come back at once."

Anne tried to maneuver the oar but it slipped in the lock. The boat drifted out further from the pier as she struggled to gain control of the small boat. "I can't get it to work."

Mary started down the path to the pier. "Take a deep breath and then pull the oar closer to your body."

But as the girl fumbled again, she let go of one of the oars and it promptly slipped into the lake. "Oh," Anne cried, immediately reaching for the oar. "Let me just."

"No," Mary called. "Don't." but it was too late. The boat tipped and Anne toppled into the water, the boat landing upside down on top of her. Mary gasped and then, not sure what else to do, dove into the water. Thank goodness, summers spent in the country meant she could swim and her light summer fashions didn't drag her down. With sure strokes she made her way to the boat diving under the water to find Anne in its murky depths. She crested once, panicking when she couldn't see the child but then a piece of fabric on the water's surface caught her attention. Anne was under the overturned boat.

Diving back in, she pushed to the rowboat, coming up and out of the water in the dark of the little boat. Anne was barely conscious, her hand loosely holding the oar as she moaned softly.

"Anne," Mary gasped grabbing the bench, to give herself a bit of respite. She reached her other hand under the girl's neck to make sure she could still breathe. "Anne, are you all right?"

"Mary?" The girl turned toward her. "I think I hit my head."

Mary pulled the girl closer. Inwardly she flinched. At least Anne was alive, but swimming the girl back was going to be challenging. And then there was Cole. He'd kept Anne tucked away doing lessons for years. One trip to the park and she'd nearly destroyed his child. "It's all right. Let's get out into the sunlight and then we'll figure out how we get to the shore.

"I don't want to let go of the boat." Anne answered.

"You don't have to. We're just going to duck under the edge while we keep holding on. Can you do that?"

Anne nodded. "I think so."

"Such a brave girl." She stroked Anne's cheek.

"You're not angry with me?"

Mary shook her head. "I would like you to proceed with more caution. Your father trusted us to be adventurers. We have to reward him with doing so in a safe manner."

Anne wrapped her free arm around Mary. "I love you."

"I love you too." She kissed the girl's head. "Now hold your breath and close your eyes. We're going under."

———

Sin arrived home to find a lovely note with scrolling handwriting in the center of his desk. The words, however, made him shift. They'd gone to the park.

Their excursion shouldn't be a big deal. And yet, he'd managed to keep Anne under his watchful eye and to have her gone...

Fortunately, Mary had given him the exact location. He breathed a sigh of relief. How did she understand he needed to know these things? He covered his heart with his hand. She'd confessed her love yesterday. He hadn't been able to say the words back, which made him hang his head in shame.

All night, as they'd dined together, laughed together, and then tucked his daughter in, he'd been tempted to say the words. "I love you, Mary. You're my salvation." But his fear held him back.

Perhaps this picnic was the perfect opportunity to rectify his mistake. After grabbing his hat, he headed for the park after them. He spotted their blanket almost immediately. First, there were no others set up but it was also the same one they'd used the day before. Glancing about, he didn't see them anywhere. And then his eyes landed on the overturned boat. No one was about. His heart seized in his chest and without another thought he threw his hat to the ground, ripping off his coat as he sprinted toward the water.

He didn't pause as he dove into the murky water and cresting the surface, he heard a small cry.

"Papa."

That made him stop. Looking ahead, he saw both Anne and Mary holding the edge of the boat. "We're all right," Mary called. "We just…"

Without a word, he began swimming for them again. He could have lost them, lost them both. How could they do this to him? But then he stopped. How much of his life would he live to avoid all the things that might go wrong? That wasn't fair to Anne or Mary. He'd been trying to protect her to the point of barely living life.

Reaching the boat, he grabbed Anne in a hug. "Mary," he gurgled out. "Put your arm about me too."

She draped her free arm about his shoulders. "I'm so sorry," she gasped. "I pushed too far. I—"

"It's my fault. I didn't listen to Mary. I won't do it again." Anne pulled back. "Papa, don't change your mind. Please marry Mary."

He shook his head. They knew him too well. "Of course I am going to marry her." He pulled back. "I love her, you know."

Both of them gasped. "You…you love me?" Mary asked.

He leaned over and kissed his fiancée. "More than I can ever say."

"You're not angry at me for this?" She looked at the boat.

"I am, a bit. And angry at myself too. I can't keep the people I love tucked away from danger always. I see that now."

Mary squeezed his shoulders. "We'll do better to keep you from worrying."

"Say. Are you all right out there?" a man called from the shore. "I can row another boat out to you."

"That is an excellent idea," Sin called back. Then he looked at Mary. "Let's be honest, my method wasn't working very well. I'm ready to try it your way."

She kissed him then, her mouth soft against his. "Thank you for that." Then she giggled, whispering close to his ear. "My way involves more than one child in our future."

He kissed her cheek. "Mary. It only took one time for me to understand there'd be no stopping you. I'm at your mercy."

EPILOGUE

Two years later...

Mary lay in her bed, tired but so satisfied, she didn't think she'd ever have a more perfect moment in her life.

In her arms lay their beautiful new baby boy. Behind her, cradling her to his chest, was her husband. He stroked her hair back from her temple as he kissed her forehead. "You made that look easy."

She chuckled. "It wasn't."

"Still. You were impressive. I...." He kissed her again. "I never imagined birth would be so beautiful."

"I never imagined you'd stay for the whole thing." She turned to capture a kiss from his lips.

He shook his head. "While I like doing things your way, I'm still me. I need to be here to make certain nothing goes awry."

"That is an excellent point." She kissed him again. "Isn't he beautiful?"

"Edward might be the most beautiful thing I've ever seen in my life, besides you, of course," he answered. "And Anne."

She rubbed her cheek on his chest. "Sometimes I think I might need to pinch myself because in my wildest dreams I never imagined my life would be like this."

"Like what?" he asked, placing his arm under hers to help support Edward.

"A fairy tale," she answered. "My happily ever after."

The baby gurgled, content at her breast as Cole rocked them both. "You're my happily ever after too, my second chance when I never thought I'd recover from the first," he said.

"So tell me." She looked up, smiling into his eyes. "Have you decided to leave my bed? I've given you your heir."

He quirked a brow. "You know very well that I am never leaving your bed. You don't have to point out what a fool I was to think it was even a possibility."

She gave a small giggle. "Sorry my love, it's just rather satisfying to know you love me and that our happy ending doesn't have an expiration."

"Fair enough. But you know I never question any of your Chase instincts. You've even won over Reeves."

Reeves had spent the last several days keeping Anne company as Mary had been too advanced in her pregnancy to do so. "He only wanted to protect you," she said. "In the end, he knows I make you happy."

He stroked the baby's head, still rocking them both. "Me and Anne. You make us both happy. You have put us back together when I thought there was no hope. Mary Sinclair, you are my everything."

Her heart nearly burst from her chest. "You're my everything too."

EARL OF GOLD

LORDS OF SCANDAL

Penny Walters sat in front of the chipped and cracked mirror attempting to assess if the style of her hair was at all pleasing. Styling herself had never been her strong suit. Even in the speckled reflection, she noted several stray curls sticking up at odd angles. She wrinkled her nose as she lifted her hands to her hair once again.

"It looks dreadful," a young voice called from the door.

She let out a long sigh, sliding out a pin. "I was afraid of that."

Her friend and companion, Clarissa, slid into the room, her bare feet sliding across the worn wood. Penny had bought her new shoes, but the girl would only wear them outside the house. Penny supposed Clarissa wasn't actually a girl anymore. At eighteen she was nearly a woman, but she was slight and small, and she padded barefoot as much as she wore footwear. She seemed so much younger than Penny even though only four years separated them.

"How long before you leave?" Clarissa asked, already pulling the rest of the pins from Penny's brown hair. It was thick and full with long waves that made it terribly unruly.

"A quarter hour," Penny answered, smiling at Clarissa in the glass. Her appointment wasn't for two hours yet, but she needed time to cross the city.

Clarissa nodded without response as she brusquely brushed out the locks. The girl had been the daughter of a country barrister before she'd been orphaned. Penny had found her at a church on her return trip from Dover six years prior. She'd been hoping to obtain a position as a governess but the family had gone with another candidate.

Directionless, Penny had been returning to London, wondering what she might do with the rest of her life. And that's when she'd found a young Clarissa. Barely old enough to care for herself, Penny hadn't been able to leave the fierce girl behind. The priest there had been attempting to convince Clarissa to join the nearby convent. An honest choice but as Clarissa was regularly blasphemous, it likely would have been an ill fit.

Now she couldn't imagine her life without her friend. Clarissa began to re-pin the hair, pins sticking out of her mouth, even as she talked. "I don't understand why you didn't just ask me to do it in the first place."

"You were helping Natty and Fran," Penny answered, her grin growing. With a few benefactors, and a small inheritance, Penny had been able to maintain her family home just outside of the Docklands and convert it to a small orphanage. The East End reeked of the tanning mills just outside the city and the paint was chipped and worn but it was all they could afford. All in all, she had four girls living with her. Ones that society would have swept under the carpet and looked away from as the mean streets ate them for breakfast.

They'd been orphaned for one reason or another and she'd determined to give each of them a real home. With food and clothes, love and shoes...

"May I ask why you aren't wearing the new boots I bought you?" She suppressed a grin as Clarissa wrinkled her nose.

"You know I don't like anything on my feet." Clarissa pulled a good deal harder than was necessary as she tamed an unruly lock of hair.

"Do they not fit?" Penny raised her brows refusing to give up the subject. She loved Clarissa like a sister which was why she needed to start wearing coverings on her feet. One could not go out and get a job or a husband while barefoot. Penny had rescued Clarissa to give her choices in life. Not to hide her away in this house.

"They fit fine," Clarissa sighed as she twisted once more. "After spending two years in shoes that were too small, I can't abide them any longer."

Penny grimaced, her smile falling from her face. Clarissa's father had lost every shilling the family had on a bad investment. He'd taken his own life and left Clarissa to face the world alone. "I'm sorry I couldn't buy new ones for you sooner."

"Don't be." Clarissa shook her head, a small jerk before she wrapped her arm about Penny's shoulders in a quick hug. The gesture was given so rarely that Penny blinked in surprise. "Natty, Fran, and Ethel needed food and books before I needed new shoes. You did what was right."

Penny sighed again, a much smaller sound as her head hung low in momentary defeat. It was difficult to find benefactors. Despite the opulence that graced the West End streets of London, here on the East End that sort of generosity was in short supply.

"So why are you meeting this new man?"

Penny gripped the table as Clarissa pulled again. She'd hoped that the Duke of Darlington would aid in her cause. This three-bedroom house fit the six of them, but she could hardly bring more children here. She needed a bigger space, more staff, and supplies for schooling if she really wanted to make a difference. "His Grace regretted to inform me that he could not personally contribute but that he had a friend that might be able to help."

Clarissa made a pishing sound as she pinned in the final curl. "So you're going to meet a man you don't know at all, and have no introduction to, alone?"

Penny's teeth clenched. "I have an introduction." She paused, seeing Clarissa's eyes harden in the mirror. "I don't have a choice." The truth was, not only did she need a benefactor to move them up in the world, they were dangerously low on funds. Acid spread in her stomach. She needed this man to agree to help her just so that they might continue to eat, and the children needed coats and…

"I could come with you." Clarissa stepped back, assessing her work. "Much better."

Penny looked in the mirror, noting that neat coif coiled in twists at her nape. Only a few pieces floated around her face to soften her features, accentuating her high cheekbones. "My hair is much better and thank you, but no. You should stay here. Natty and Fran need you."

Clarissa frowned. "We could all go. Wait in the carriage."

Penny looked down at the floor. She didn't plan to take a carriage. The address the duke had given her was on the west side, of course, but she'd walk. A hack would take valuable shillings they didn't have. Inside, she sighed again but she didn't allow Clarissa to hear her this time. Life was often difficult these days. And Clarissa was too young to help her bear that burden. "I'll be fine, Clarissa. Keep working with the girls on their letters. And put on your shoes."

"Why?" Clarissa sniffed, turning back toward the door.

"I've told you why. You need them to move on from us and live your life and—"

Clarissa wrinkled her nose. "I already have a job and a life. I educate the little ones. And I'm not getting married. You need me too much."

And just like that, Clarissa was gone again.

It would be easier if that girl weren't right so often. And how did Clarissa know she wouldn't marry? Penny, despite the independent steps she'd taken, still sometimes wished for a husband to share her burden and provide a family of her own. But then she shook her head. That was never going to happen. She was already a spinster and her life was entrenched in these children's needs. Still, sometimes she dreamed...

Penny rose and left her room, almost conceding and taking Clarissa. The company would be nice. She had a hard exterior, Clarissa, but underneath that was a soft heart. And Penny loved her for it.

Putting on her pelisse, she ignored the threadbare appearance as she buttoned it against the sharp fall wind. Then she set off, exiting her home and starting down the street. It would be a long walk. She looked at the slip of paper that held the name and address of the potential benefactor. The Earl of Goldthwaite. What an interesting name.

She could only hope he was the sort of man with a generous spirit and giving nature and that was why the duke had sent her to meet him.

———

Shadows were falling about the London streets when Logan finally returned home. He'd spent the afternoon in a series of Gentleman's Clubs looking for potential partners. The search had proven fruitless.

The men he'd met were either nitwits, had no head for business, or an appetite for nothing but leisure. It didn't help that he couldn't outright tell them about the club. The sword of secrecy had made communication near impossible.

Now he wished for a bath, a meal, and bed—in that order. Of course, the stack of work that waited on his desk would have to be attended. Daring's assignment was proving problematic already and for a brief moment, he considered leaving the venture all together. While he knew he could manage the work, the business of working with others might prove too difficult…

"My lord," his butler greeted him at the front door, giving his employer a sharp frown of disapproval. "You've a visitor."

"What?" he gritted out as he shrugged off his coat. He ignored the judgment from the other man, accustomed to his butler's clucking nature. But what surprised him was the announcement that some person had come calling. No one visited him…ever. Unless it was his solicitor. All other business ventures were always conducted in neutral territory. An office, a club, or some such place.

It was part of his strategy. People were more comfortable in their own spaces, which was often an advantage.

The man's eyebrows rose in what looked to be mild condemnation. "Miss Penny Walters. She had an appointment several hours ago. I encouraged her to reschedule, but she insisted on waiting."

His eyes briefly closed before they snapped open again. Shit. He'd forgotten. Which was unlike him, but why in the bloody blue blazes would she stay all this time? Ridiculous.

And now he had far too much to do for how bone-tired he was. The last thing he needed was to delicately remove a female from his residence. "Where is she?"

"The front sitting room," Winter responded, "Where she has waited with an excessive amount of patience." Then the man folded his hands in front of him, his mouth turning down a bit deeper at the corners. His eyes gave the accusation his mouth had not.

Logan's face hardened. Could this day get any worse? Was his own butler judging him now? The man was a bit unconventional, but he'd always been respectful.

Logan made an abrupt turn and started for the sitting room, annoyance hot under his collar. He had no temper for this meeting.

The door was slightly ajar, and he pushed it open with a satisfying bang, entering into the darkening room with all the subtlety of a herd of stampeding cattle. The gesture was meant to be less than welcoming and more like a clear message to get the hell out. He didn't have the patience to be delicate.

The day had been beyond frustrating.

But if he'd frightened Miss Penny Walters with his display, she showed no sign. Her face was turned toward the window, her posture perfectly upright, her hands neatly folded in her lap. Her figure was trim, that was what he noticed first in the light spilling in from the hall. Very slowly, she turned to look at him, her features illuminated in the most breathtaking way.

He locked his gaze on her large eyes, fringed with long dark lashes. Then he lowered his gaze to take in her small straight nose, accented by high cheekbones and lush full lips. If he were honest, she stole his breath. Which was most likely why he'd yet to utter a word despite his grand entrance.

"Lord Goldthwaite?" she asked, rising slowly from her chair.

If he'd come in like a blustering idiot, she was the picture of seren-ity. Not that she filled him with calm. Because he realized, while she was trim she was also quite…curvy. Delightfully so. His gut clenched as his body responded. Was her hair as dark and as full as it appeared or was that the dim light?

"Yes," he said after a moment's hesitation.

She began crossing toward him, a smile on her face as she reached out a hand. She showed no sign of irritation that she'd been kept waiting for hours. "I'm very pleased to meet you. I am Miss Penny Walters and—"

"I know who you are." His voice grated out. Was that his irritation or was it his desire that made him sound so guttural?

Her smile slipped for just a moment before she placed it firmly back in place. "A pleasure to meet you."

He didn't take her hand. "What are you doing here?"

She folded her hands once again. Her shoulders remained straight, her back stiff as she continued to smile. How did she maintain such sunny calm? His gaze flitted down her body once again. He couldn't seem to help himself, but her words drew his eyes back up to hers.

"We had an appointment," she said.

"My lord," Winters called behind him. "May I enter to light more candles?"

Logan snapped his teeth together. "We don't need candles. We won't be long." Truth be told, he wasn't certain he wanted to see this woman in any more detail. Would she be as beautiful as he imagined or was partial shadow her friend? It was best he didn't find out.

"Mr. Winters," Miss Walters called. "Perhaps just one."

The damn man slid behind him, crossing and lighting a candle just next to Miss Penny Walters.

He straightened up with a breath of irritation. What happening that she'd usurped him in his own house? It was on the tip of his tongue to tell the man to get out of the room. For that matter, the man could leave the house entirely. But the words died on his lips.

Because Mr. Winters had never been a normal butler and Logan was used to the man, he supposed.

But he soon forgot all about his errant butler. Because bloody hell if Miss Walters wasn't even more lovely with added light. "Mr. Winters, after Miss Walters is gone, you and I need to have a chat."

"Of course, my lord," the man answered, sounding wholly unconcerned. Then the butler left again without another word.

Penny cleared her throat. He studied her again and noted that while her features were as stunning as he'd first imagined, her clothing left a great deal to be desired. Threadbare, her dress looked as though it had been mended several times. His little Penny was as poor as her name implied.

"My lord, you're right of course. I only need a moment of your time."

"How much?" he asked, crossing his arms.

"I beg your pardon. How much of what? Time? As I said, just a moment," she said, her brows drawing together.

Her hand trembled ever so slightly, betraying her nerves. Somehow that knowledge helped him relax. She wasn't as immune to him as he'd first believed. He leaned against the door jamb, one foot kicking in front of the other. She'd unsettled him after a long day and her calm had further made him feel inferior.

He'd been an ass for forgetting their meeting, he knew that. But he was also the one with the fat purse. He could afford to be ill-mannered. She could not, he thought dryly.

"How much money do you need for your orphanage?" he asked, crossing his arms. Best to move her out as quickly as possible and now that he thought about it, he might feel better to have accomplished one of Daring's two goals so quickly. He was glad she'd stayed after all.

"Well," she paused "One thousand five hundred pounds—"

"Done," he said before she could finish.

One of her brows quirked. "Annually should suffice for this first house."

His teeth ground together. "Three thousand pounds this one time and I want my name on the front plaque of the orphanage."

She shook her head. "The sum is very generous but without an annual income, I cannot afford the plaque because there will be no orphanage."

He scrubbed his face then. "Try to understand, Miss Walters, that a one-time sum is all I am willing to contribute." It would fulfill Daring's request and allow him to move forward with the deal. That was all he really cared about.

She let out a sigh, her bosom rising in the most alluring way. "Very well. But you'll have to provide the plaque yourself."

Want to read more? Earl of Gold can be found on all major retailers!

Keep up with all the latest news, sales, freebies, and releases by joining my newsletter!

www.tammyandresen.com

Hugs!

OTHER TITLES BY TAMMY

The Dark Duke's Legacy

Her Wicked White

Her Wanton White

His Wallflower White

Her Willful White

Her Wanton White

His White Wager

Her White Wedding

Lords of Scandal

Duke of Daring

Marquess of Malice

Earl of Exile

Viscount of Vice

Baron of Bad

Earl of Sin

Earl of Gold

Earl of Baxter

Duke of Decandence

Marquess of Menace

Duke of Dishonor

Baron of Blasphemy

Viscount of Vanity

Earl of Infamy

Laird of Longing

The Dark Duke's Legacy

Her Wicked White

Her Willful White

His Wallflower White

Her Wanton White

Her Wild White

His White Wager

Her White Wedding

The Rake's Ruin

When only an Indecent Duke Will Do

How to Catch an Elusive Earl

Where to Woo a Bawdy Baron

When a Marauding Marquess is Best

What a Vulgar Viscount Needs

Who Wants a Brawling Baron

When to Dare a Dishonorable Duke

The Wicked Wallflowers

Earl of Dryden

Too Wicked to Woo

Too Wicked to Wed

Too Wicked to Want

How to Reform a Rake

Don't Tell a Duke You Love Him

Meddle in a Marquess's Affairs

Never Trust an Errant Earl

Never Kiss an Earl at Midnight

Make a Viscount Beg

Fairfield Fairy Tales

Stealing a Lady's Heart

Hunting for a Lady's Heart

Entrapping a Lord's Love: Coming in February of 2018

American Historical Romance

Lily in Bloom

Midnight Magic

The Golden Rules of Love

Boxsets!!

Taming the Duke's Heart Books 1-3

American Brides

A Laird to Love

Wicked Lords of London

ABOUT THE AUTHOR

Tammy Andresen lives with her husband and three children just outside of Boston, Massachusetts. She grew up on the Seacoast of Maine, where she spent countless days dreaming up stories in blueberry fields and among the scrub pines that line the coast. Her mother loved to spin a yarn and Tammy filled many hours listening to her mother retell the classics. It was inevitable that at the age of eighteen, she headed off to Simmons College, where she studied English literature and education. She never left Massachusetts but some of her heart still resides in Maine and her family visits often.

Find out more about Tammy:
http://www.tammyandresen.com/
https://www.facebook.com/authortammyandresen
https://twitter.com/TammyAndresen
https://www.pinterest.com/tammy_andresen/
https://plus.google.com/+TammyAndresen/

Printed in Great Britain
by Amazon

41592043R00057